The Promise

The Promise

Living A Meaningful Life

by
Brian Hunter

*Published by
Wizard Way
Rainbow Wisdom
Ireland*

Copyright © 2022 Brian Hunter

All rights reserved.
No part of this publication may be reproduced, stored in a retrieval system, or transmitted, in any form or by any means, electronic, mechanical, photocopying, recording or otherwise. without the prior permission of *Rainbow Wisdom*

This book is sold subject to the condition that it shall not, by way of trade or otherwise, be lent, re-sold, hired out, or otherwise circulated without the publisher's prior consent in any form of binding or cover other than that in which it is published and without a similar condition including this condition being imposed on the subsequent purchaser.

ISBN: 9798404027600

Cover photography by
Anastasia Krachkovskaya

www.ottawagraphics.com

www.brianhunterauthor.com

DEDICATION

This book is dedicated to all of those who put children before themselves, knowing that our children are our most important investment and biggest hope for the future.

CONTENTS

	PREFACE	7
1	The Return	9
2	The Christmas	57
3	The Wedding	100
4	The Dork	138
	Acknowledgments	172
	About The Author	173
	Also, by Brian Hunter	174
	Living A Meaningful Life: Series Synopsis	176

PREFACE

The Promise is Book #5 in the series, "Living A Meaningful Life," by Brian Hunter. *The Promise* is a highly meaningful and powerful book in its' own right. But to better understand some of the storylines, back-stories, and context, it is highly recommended that you first read the prior books in the series:

Book #1: *The Bench: Living A Meaningful Life*

Book #2: *The Farm: Living A Meaningful Life*

Book #3: *The Lake: Living A Meaningful Life*

Book #4: *The Favor: Living A Meaningful Life*

Book #5: *The Promise: Living A Meaningful Life*

Book #6: *The Sacrifice: Living A Meaningful Life*

Book #7: *The Challenge: Living A Meaningful Life*

Book #8: *The Wedding: Living A Meaningful Life*

Book #9: *The Crew: Living A Meaningful Life*

Book #10: *The Substitute: Living A Meaningful Life*

Book #11: *The Graduate: Living A Meaningful Life*

Book #12: *The Nemesis: Living A Meaningful Life*

Book #13: *The Proposal: Living A Meaningful Life*

Book #14: *The Estate: Living A Meaningful Life*

Book #15: *The Heir: Living A Meaningful Life*

Book #16: *The Renaissance: Living A Meaningful Life*

Book #17: *The Shelton: Living A Meaningful Life*

Book #18: *The Ramone: Living A Meaningful Life*

Book #19: *The Spare: Living A Meaningful Life*
Book #20: *The Gala: Living A Meaningful Life*
Book #21: *The Commencement: Living A Meaningful Life*
Book #22: *The Bank: Living A Meaningful Life*
Book #23: *The Dean: Living A Meaningful Life*
Book #24: *The Key: Living A Meaningful Life*
Book #25: *The Hospital: Living A Meaningful Life*
Book #26: *The Lieutenant: Living A Meaningful Life*
Book #27: *The Flashback: Living A Meaningful Life*
Book #28: *The Promotion: Living A Meaningful Life*

CHAPTER ONE
The Return

After the amazing, heartbreaking, earth-shaking life-changing, sad, joyful, inspiring, and immense carnage experienced by honoring 'the favor' out of respect and love for Frank, I had finally arrived back to my life in Los Angeles.

I had been in an exhausted trance for the entire flight, and then fell deep into a state of contemplative reflection while staring down at the grandeur of southern California as we descended for landing into LAX.

As we made the approach into the airport, the sun was setting. I found myself admiring the beauty of the incredible sunset over Los Angeles, just as I had been emotionally attached to all of the sunsets back home at the farm. However, the sunset over LA seemed to have a different meaning than those at the farm. At the farm, sunsets were a major point of the day, where I would stop to reflect upon what things of meaning I had accomplished. They were about the pure beauty of simply existing and living. At the farm, I LIVED the sunsets. In contrast, the sunsets in LA were more of a sight of beauty to 'consume,' as part of the excitement and allure of living in the place that never sleeps and is always reaching for unreachable dreams.

Before I had even landed, I was realizing which was more meaningful, and which was not so much. Still the same, I was excited to be going back to where I had been so happy for three years, before the phone call from Frank that pulled me away. Perhaps after being back in LA for a while, I could find that same happiness again?

After retrieving my luggage and a taxi ride to my apartment, I entered my old, tiny, 'dump' of an apartment. I turned on the light and just stood there, looking around my tiny space I called 'home' when in LA. It was very surreal for numerous reasons. First of all, EVERYTHING was EXACTLY as I had left it. This might not seem like a surprise since I lived alone and nobody had entered my apartment while I was gone, but it was weird to me because so much had changed in life while I was away. My life was completely different in almost every way. Yet, the inside of my apartment was like a huge time capsule which I was experiencing in real-time. I saw my research paper for college still laying out on my desk just as I had left it. I looked at my wall calendar, which was open to the page from many months ago when I left. On it were things written like, "mountain hike" on certain days, and "Santa Monica" for another day, and also listings of when my exams for school were scheduled. I had missed all of them. I had not done a single thing that was scheduled on my calendar.

I looked around my apartment at my old couch, my table that I had snatched from the dumpster outside, my beach shorts and sweats that were my only wardrobe in LA, my old pots and pans, and my pantry full of soup and ramen. My refrigerator was full of old salsa that needed to be thrown out, and there was an empty pizza box still sitting by the trash that never got thrown out before I left.

I was looking at the apartment of a young college student who had no money, no outside life, ate fast food, and whose only thoughts of the world consisted of school and leisure. My mind was struggling to decide whether I was looking at an apartment of a completely different person from before the phone call, or if my mind was deciding if the recent events and reality of who I had now become, what had happened, and how much responsibility and money I now had, were all just part of a delusional dream that wasn't real.

One thing for sure was that I couldn't reconcile the two lives, between my life before going back home, and my life after having been back home. Everything seemed too different. Aside from my unfathomable losses, along with the blessings of my new life, I was trying deep inside to reconnect with my carefree happiness that I had felt before Frank's phone call.

For this reason, I guess my mind decided that it wanted to pretend that my new reality was nothing more than a delusional dream that had never happened. With that decision made, I settled back into my apartment as if I was completely comfortable in it. And guess what? After about an hour or so, I *was* completely comfortable in it. Yeah, it was small, old, and even dismal; but it was where I had felt my carefree happiness. That is what I wanted most at that moment. I wanted my carefree happiness back. Thus, I decided to just roll with my old lifestyle as if nothing new had ever happened.

While on the airplane, I had some thoughts of upgrading my living situation to a nicer apartment more befitting of my new budget. But after being back in my old apartment, I discarded that notion. I decided that I was comfortable there, and it was the place that I had known for three years during some of my happiest or most 'content' years.

I decided to order a pizza, as I had often done before. My pizza arrived, and it never tasted so good as it did then. I was already happier. I cleaned my place up a little, and set my school research paper out of the way. I unpacked my suitcase and put everything back where it belonged. I watched TV that night for the first time in many months. Not once had I watched TV while back home. Not a single time. Frank had a TV, but he never used it, and I am not even sure it worked because we never turned it on.

After watching a couple of my TV shows, which I was hopelessly behind on, I went to bed. I never slept so good in my life. I think it was because I was completely alone, was not submerged in trauma, had no distractions, and I had zero responsibilities the next morning. I didn't have to wake up early for chores, or for meetings, or for breakfast, or for anything. There was NOTHING for me to do the next day. Was that good? Or was that not good? I couldn't decide how to answer that question.

I slept undisturbed until I woke up naturally much later in the morning than I was used to. Looking at the time I woke up, plus the time zone difference, I calculated that Eric would have already done all of the farm chores, and would be sitting down for lunch. Eric would have already lived much of the day, while I had only just woken up. Was this good? Or was this bad? Was I lucky to have been able to sleep in? Or was I not?

I decided to go for a morning walk at the beach. The sun was out, everything was beautiful, and all was calm. It was a perfect southern California day. The ocean was smooth, the beach was mostly empty, and the smell of the ocean air was refreshing. But I was alone. I was walking alone. To where? Nowhere. I was going nowhere, with no purpose. I was just walking to walk.

I loved the sun on my face and the air I was breathing. But I was alone with no responsibilities, no chores, no tasks, and seemingly no purpose, other than to chase some old ghost of how I used to feel before Frank's phone call.

I spent my first few days just "existing," as opposed to LIVING. I felt comfortable back inside my old apartment, and decided to continue living there, even though it was a dump, and I didn't have to live in a dump anymore if I didn't want to. It was bizarre, but it was as if my bank account didn't exist in California. I found myself living as modestly as before. I was checking the prices on all of the food I was buying, and I was careful to continue conserving my utility use as I had always done. Apparently, I had decided to go back to living my old life, including my old budgetary constraints.

I think I wanted to try and live as closely as possible to how I had lived before Frank's call, in hopes that I could find that 'happy place' which I had been experiencing before Frank's call.

The only time I got pulled back into my true reality was when Jonathan called me. As soon as I started speaking with Jonathan, I would snap back into my actual reality. I would act like, think like, and BE the person that I had become after everything happened. But once I hung up with Jonathan, I would immediately revert back to the person I WAS, before I became what I became.

Was I developing a split personality disorder or something? I was living two different versions of myself, and I think my mind was trying to decide which version was the more real version of myself, and which was the better version.

After a couple weeks of this, I asked myself what I was doing there. I didn't have a good answer that felt authentic; but I latched onto the idea that I was there to resume my studies at the university, and finish my degree as Frank had wanted. That was something solid and certain that I felt I could use as a foundation for why I was in California.

I decided to pull myself together and try to put some purpose back into my life. I made some inquiries with the university about starting up again, and they were happy to work with me and accommodate this.

So, I guess I was going to be going back to school again. No more days of just doing nothing in my apartment. Was this a good thing, or a bad thing?

It was shortly after that, for the first time, that I agreed to acknowledge my new bank account, although just for a fleeting moment. This happened when I thought of driving back and forth from classes again in my old unreliable and broken car.

I may have been satisfied with staying in my old, tiny, and dumpy apartment eating cheap fast food or soup, but I was NOT satisfied dealing with that old car again. NOPE. Not happening!

So, I broke down and decided to reach into the pockets of the other version of myself that had more money. I drove my desperate and dying car to the local car dealership.

Upon arrival, the car salesman took a look at me, a college student dressed in beach shorts with an old broken-down car, and he snooted his nose up and asked how he could help me.

I had already decided what I wanted to buy before I arrived. I had settled on getting a nice SUV, but nothing fancy. I just wanted a simple common vehicle that was brand new and would never break down on the freeway.

I told the salesperson what I wanted, and that I wanted a white one. He looked over at my current car in disgust and asked if *that* was my trade-in. I told him that I didn't want to take it back home again, if that answered his question.

He took me over to the vehicle I had described, including the correct color of white. I looked it over, inside and out. It was what I wanted. I said to him, "I'll take it."

He responded by saying, "Don't you want to test drive it first?"

I replied, "No. It's brand new. It's under warranty. If it's trash, I will just bring it back to you. I'll test drive it on the way home after I buy it."

He looked at me weird. Perhaps he thought this was a prank and I was not there to really buy a car. Regardless, he walked me back over to the office, and led me inside. We sat down at his desk, and he wrote a bunch of numbers on his paper. He showed me what they would give me for my car, and what the new one would be, along with my financing options.

He then said, "This is assuming you have good credit. If you don't, none of this will work. Do you have any credit, Sir?"

I replied, "No, actually I don't."

He sighed in frustration, as if I was just wasting his time. He said, "With no credit, there is no way you can buy this vehicle."

Now *I* was the one becoming annoyed, and I looked at him and said, "Why? Don't you guys take cash anymore? Doesn't money buy cars?"

He looked at *me*, looked out the window at my awful car, then looked back at me again, and said, "Are you telling me that *you* will be paying cash?"

I replied, "Yes, that is what I am telling you, Sir."

He looked at me like he almost wanted to ask me to throw it all on his desk to prove it first. But instead, he just gave me a funny look and started writing up a new paper. He showed me some numbers.

I told him he could have my old car for free, but I wanted a certain discount on the new one because obviously I wasn't paying full price.

He changed the numbers to reflect this. I was okay with what he showed me. I told him I would agree to that.

He then asked where the cash was. I told him I had to get it from my car. I got up and walked out to my old car. I had stuffed a paper bag full of cash under my seat. I grabbed it, along with my few personal things left in the car, and I walked back into his office. I set the paper bag containing the cash on his desk. I told him we would need to count it out for the correct amount. I then picked up the paper bag, flipped it upside down, and dumped all of the bundled cash out onto his desk.

He looked at me like I was some kind of Columbian drug lord or something. He started counting the cash as I was watching. He counted out the correct amount that was needed, and I agreed he did it correctly, unless he was good at sleight-of-hand magic tricks or something. He pushed the leftover cash back over to me, and I stuffed it back inside the worn paper bag.

I filled out a bunch of paperwork, and so did he. Finally, we were done. He gave me the keys, and he congratulated me on my new car in a very fake salesman type way. I thanked him and walked out, carrying my bag of leftover cash. I climbed into my brand-new vehicle, stuffed my bag of cash under the seat, and drove home. Once I was back home, I completely forgot about my bank account again, and I resumed my life as a poor college student with no money.

That new vehicle would be my only extravagant purchase for myself in quite a long time. I was satisfied with everything else. OH, except my old frying pan. I bought a new pan for the rare occasions when I cooked something like eggs or steak. A really nice pan. But that's it. Nothing else. Just the car and the frying pan.

I started back at the university immediately. I was starting two weeks late, so I had to play catch-up. I was totally focused on school for about three weeks before I was caught up and was in a comfortable routine with school.

Life was really busy for me again. I was waking up earlier in the morning so that I could talk with Jonathan. Early morning was the best time for my phone meetings with him because of the time zone difference. This way, I took care of my business obligations early; and then after my classes, I could be done with everything for the day, and do whatever I wanted after that.

My days became very routine and structured. It was Jonathan early in the morning, day full of classes, then my early evening run along the greenbelt, followed by dinner. After that, I would do school work, or look over papers for The Carlisle Trust so that I could be prepared for my morning meeting with Jonathan. If I had time, I would watch TV before bed. However, I found myself not having as much time for TV anymore. My obligations with The Carlisle Trust were no joke and were quite time consuming. I took both of my obligations to The Carlisle Trust and to school very seriously. I didn't cut corners on either one. Thus, my previous college life of leisure which I had lived before was no longer a possible reality anyway, despite my best efforts to return to my old life.

After I had caught up with school and got into an efficient routine with keeping up with The Carlisle Trust work, I started resuming my weekend activities. I began going for random hikes again and partaking in my beach days.

There was one particular beach day when I was hit by a wave of contradictory feelings, doubts, and misgivings. It was a nice enough day, and I enjoyed a wonderful walk on the strand that went along the beach and the mansions. But when I went out onto the quiet beach to sit for a while, I started having serious thoughts and questions of what in the world I was doing there.

What WAS I DOING there???

Why was I sitting on a beach all alone in California? Why was I going to college? Why was I living so far away from my real life? Did I just admit that my "real life" was not in California? If so, then why was I not living where my real life was? What was I trying to prove? What was I trying to accomplish?

It all started to feel so ridiculous to me being there. Everything that mattered to me was back home. The farm, Eric, The Carlisle Trust, Rudy, Trevor and Heather, Mr. Wilkens' house, the park, the bench, the 'real' sunsets, the sunrises that I loved there but never noticed in LA, and even the community of people who were beginning to respect and rely upon my leadership to make things better. The high school, and the kids at the high school, were needing me to make things better for them. I had huge, important, and meaningful responsibilities back home. Why was I sitting on a beach all alone in California? What was I trying to accomplish or prove by going to college, when my future and career were already clearly mapped out and locked in?

These realizations were starting to make me feel irresponsible. Was I trying to dodge or avoid the realities of my life by hiding out in California and pretending I was just a college kid? Why was I pretending I was just a poor college kid? Doing that would be a lie.

I was lying to myself and everyone else. I wasn't a poor college kid. I was someone who held a very important position, who did very important work for lots of people who were counting on me. Why was I hiding in California and pretending that the importance of my position and work didn't exist?

Did Mrs. Carlisle and Frank teach me to live in denial within a fake alternate universe? I don't think so. So why was I? Was I letting everyone down by sitting out on that beach all alone? Was I bringing shame to myself and the values which The Carlisle Trust stood for? Was I setting a bad example for Eric, Jonathan, and everyone who looked to me for leadership and guidance?

Was this California existence just a way for me to avoid my own true reality? Was going to college just my way of pretending that everything that happened, didn't happen? Was this like when you're struggling as a teenager, so you pretend you're a little child again? Was I pretending to be a little child again? Was I just a young, fresh-faced, poor college student starting out in life? Did the fact I stayed living in a dumpy little apartment prove to myself that I was still just a kid going to school, with nothing, and no important responsibilities?

I tortured myself for a couple of hours with all of these thoughts before I gave up on having a peaceful enjoyable afternoon. I got up from the sand, and went back home. Once I was home, I saw all of my school work sitting on my desk. This caused me to snap out of my funk and refocus on my school work. I convinced myself that if for no other reason, I needed to focus on school until school was done. After all, it was FRANK who INSISTED that I get my business degree. It wasn't my idea. It was FRANK'S. So, if Frank insisted on it, then that is what I should be doing. Right?

So, I guess it was settled! I was in California to get my business degree as Frank had wanted. I almost felt like writing that on pieces of paper and taping the papers all over my apartment so that I would never forget my purpose there. The reason why was because I would often still have those thoughts of being in the wrong place. I still had my thoughts of being irresponsible for living out there. Perhaps I needed to constantly remind myself of why I was there?

I even said to myself a couple of times, "You belong here," when standing in my apartment. My reaction after saying that phrase was to laugh. I didn't belong there, and I knew it. Even so, I continued living my conflicted California school beach life for more weeks to come. I made it into November, and I even informed Eric and my parents that I would not be going back home for Thanksgiving. My reasoning was that I didn't want to travel all of that distance for only four days. It was easier for me to stay in California and keep up with my school work, and then I would fly back home for the Christmas holiday as I had always done. However, that plan was not to be. None of what I thought would happen was to be. Pretty much none of it at all, period.

It was about two weeks before Thanksgiving. I was sitting at my desk in my apartment working on a research paper for school, of all things. The phone rang. It was Eric. He sounded a bit frantic.

Eric explained that he had received a phone call from Rudy's mother. Eric mentioning Rudy was enough for me to drop my pencil and cause the hair on the back of my neck to stand on end. I listened very intently.

Eric explained that Rudy's mother had called him to say that she was having serious health problems, and would be needing to stay in the hospital for an extended period of time for treatments. She told Eric that she didn't know what to do with Rudy, and that I had told her to call him (Eric) if there was ever a problem with Rudy.

Rudy's mom wondered if there was any way that Rudy could stay at the farm for a short time, and if someone could inform *me* of what was going on. She seemed lost and desperate to make sure that Rudy would have a good and safe place to be while she was in the hospital for who knows how long.

After Eric explained everything to me, he asked me what I wanted him to do. I said to him, "Tell her you will take Rudy. Tell her that I will come there in a day or so and will take care of Rudy. Tell her that I will have Jonathan from my office call her for further assistance. Tell her that she has my full support, and that I will take full responsibility for Rudy and all of his care until she is finished with her treatments."

Eric listened without interrupting, but when I was finished, he said, "Oh my God, you are coming back in the middle of a school semester again?"

I replied, "Absolutely."

Then I said, "Get Rudy. Expect my arrival late tomorrow."

Eric responded, "Got it. Will do."

I ended my call with Eric. I immediately called Jonathan. I explained the situation. I asked him to contact Rudy's mom and offer our help. Jonathan pondered and told me that we should be getting a medical contingency order or something, which would give me emergency custody authorization to care for Rudy in the event of a medical emergency.

To be honest, I was not sure what he was talking about, or if he was talking about emergencies for Rudy's mom, or for Rudy, or what. I had begun to lose my mind in the frantic drama of the situation.

I just said to him, "Jonathan, this is where I trust you to do all of the right things. Just do whatever you know needs to be done."

Jonathan replied, "Yes, Sir."

I told Jonathan to book my travel back home for the next day, and early if possible. He acknowledged, and said he would work on all of that stuff. I ended my call with Jonathan.

I paused to take a moment with myself. I stared down at my

research paper that I was working on for school, which was due to be turned in soon.

I stood up from my desk, went into my closet, and pulled out an empty box. I brought the box back to my desk. With one hand, I swiped my hand across my desk, pushing everything, the research paper, the pencils, the pens, my notes, my school notepad, everything, into the box below. Once all of my school stuff was pushed into the box, I went and got some packing tape. I taped up the box. I wrote on the box with a marker, "College." Then I carried the sealed box into my bedroom closet and placed it in the far rear of my closet.

I returned to my desk, and then called the university office. I informed them that I was officially withdrawing from school (again). Guess how long I hesitated before doing this? Zero seconds. That's how long.

They asked me when I could return. I replied, "Maybe never," and I thanked the lady for a wonderful life experience, and told her that I had thoroughly enjoyed my life as a university student at their school.

I packed my suitcase. I received the information from Jonathan for my flight back home. I would fly out first thing in the morning.

I went for a walk on the beach as I always did whenever I left LA for a trip. I breathed in all of the ocean air, and held it within me for as long as possible, hoping to always remember it and keep it with me.

I looked at the lonely empty beach. I knew that I no longer wanted to sit alone on that lonely empty beach. I didn't belong there.

I ordered one last pizza using a $3 coupon toward the purchase, which I hadn't used yet. I enjoyed it tremendously. I cleaned up my apartment, and organized everything as if I would not be returning for a long time. I made sure all of the garbage was taken out, and that all of the food in the refrigerator was thrown out. I made sure my vehicle was locked and secured in the garage. When I felt everything was taken care of, I relaxed and watched one last TV show, and then I went to bed.

My alarm woke me up, and I got ready for my trip. Jonathan had a car from a limo service pick me up. No taxi. Limo service. That was my *real* life. It was time to own up to my life and act like it was my life. I had pretended and lived in denial long enough. My days of being a poor little college student were over. It was time to act like the responsible adult I was, in the position I was in, and honor all of those people who were counting on me, such as Rudy.

After I arrived at the airport, I noticed that Jonathan had booked me into first-class. I usually flew coach. Jonathan claimed that there were no coach seats left. However, when I was boarding the plane, I saw lots of empty coach seats.

My flight seemed fairly short back home. I had lots of things racing in my mind. I was very concerned about Rudy's mom, and about Rudy. However, I also had some moments to think about the life I had been living in LA. I thought about how I had just withdrawn from school for the second time in the middle of a semester. I admitted to myself that I was not going back. This resulted in the epiphany that I was officially a college dropout. I laughed. The lady sitting next to me must have thought I was crazy.

I landed at the airport back home. I had quite a long car ride still to come. Jonathan had another limo service car waiting for me at the airport. Finally though, I was on my way back home to the farm. It felt right. I knew I was doing the right thing, and that I was in the right place.

The car pulled into the driveway at the farm. Before I even got out of the car, I could see Rudy's cute little face looking out the dining room window, as if he had been standing there waiting for who knows how long.

Before I could fully get out of the car, Rudy had run out to me. He attacked me with his embrace, and almost knocked me over. We hugged for a good long time. He wasn't really crying, but perhaps he was close to it.

While we were hugging, I said, "It's going to be okay now, Son. I'm here with you until it's okay again."

Rudy broke his grip, looked up at me, and smiled.

Trevor ran outside and gave me a big hug also. Then he grabbed my suitcase and ran ahead inside with it.

Eric came outside, smiled at me, and said, "We meet again."

We hugged. Eric led me inside the house, where I was promptly greeted to another hug from Heather. She asked if I was hungry, and I replied, "I know I missed dinner here, but yes I am."

Heather had obviously anticipated this, and had already fixed a dinner just for me. Everyone sat down at the dining room table to watch me eat. When I was about to take my first bite, Eric put up his hand to stop me. I hesitated, and then Eric looked at me, and said, "YOU belong here."

I chuckled and replied, "Yes I do. I know that now."

Everyone watched me eat. I knew there were some serious issues to discuss and deal with regarding Rudy and his mom, but for a moment at least, I just enjoyed the fact that I was back home, and I was musing to myself at how 'RIGHT' it felt.

Rudy sat glued next to me during the entire time I ate. I knew that I had to have a long and serious discussion with him at some point, and ask him what he knew of the situation, and how he felt about everything. But during my dinner, he seemed calm and content, so I decided not to dredge up any feelings and issues that evening.

However, I wanted to speak with Eric after dinner privately. I had missed him and his counsel, and we always had a routine of reconnecting and getting caught up whenever I was back home.

When I was done eating, I looked over at Rudy and said, "You and I will have a long talk tomorrow, okay?"

Rudy replied, "Yes, I know."

Then I said, "Tonight I need to speak with Eric about some things, okay?"

Rudy replied, "Yes, okay."

Heather and Trevor also took that as their signal to allow Eric and I some time alone. Rudy, Trevor, and Heather went into the kitchen. I motioned for Eric to join me in the living room next to the fireplace. Heather was AMAZING and remembered, and knew, that I loved having some hot tea (Earl Grey) by the fireplace in the evening. She brought it right out to me before I could even remember that I wanted it. Eric and I settled into our chairs by the fire. Eric looked at me, waiting for me to say something.

All I could think of to say was, "*Holy shit*, I don't know if I am more freaked out by what is going on with Rudy and his mom, or if I am just incredibly delighted to be back home after what was quite a lonely and underwhelming stay in LA."

Eric replied, "You didn't like being back there?"

I responded, "I loved being back there. And I was lonely and slightly miserable the entire time."

Eric chuckled.

I said, "It just wasn't right. I can't explain it. It was like when you have an outfit that fit perfectly and felt awesome in the past, but then a couple of years later, it doesn't fit anymore and is very uncomfortable to wear."

Eric replied, "Well, it's not your life anymore."

I responded, "Correct. But it was a life I loved. And now it's not my life anymore, and no longer fits me. It felt wrong. It felt like I was forcing or faking it the entire time."

Eric replied, "How long can you be away from school; and what are you going to do about that?"

I responded, "I withdrew from the university. Again. But this time for good."

After a pause, I added, "I'm a college dropout, Eric."

I continued, "What kind of example does that set for everyone in this community, such as the kids in school, that I'm a college dropout? The head of The Carlisle Trust is a college dropout."

Eric replied, "You are being all crazy and delusional again. Nobody cares that you were at a university in California. In fact, everyone was wondering why in the world you were at a university out in California in the first place, instead of remaining in your community."

I responded, "Good point."

Eric replied, "You clearly are not aware of this yet, but you are the most influential person in this entire community. Nobody is going to question your choice to leave college, especially under the circumstances of why you left."

I responded, "I am clearly NOT the most influential person in this community."

Eric replied, "Why do you say that?"

I responded, "I just dropped everything I was doing, withdrew from a university, became a college dropout, and ran all the way across the country, all because of a child. I would say *that* proves that the boy attached to me at dinner this evening, and lurking around waiting for me to finish speaking to you now is the most influential person in this entire community."

Eric chuckled and replied, "Good point."

Eric hesitated a bit, and then said, "Frank is not here to say to you what you need to be told, so I am going to say it for him."

I looked at Eric inquisitively, as he rarely spoke to me in that way.

Eric said, "It's time that you pull your head out of your ass and realize how important you are to this community. It's okay to OWN your importance. Nobody is going to call you arrogant. You are anything but arrogant. But people EXPECT strength and leadership out of you. You need to start delivering that, instead of worrying about what people will think of you."

I just stared at him.

I responded, "I think Frank has invaded you and possessed your mind. That is precisely what Frank would say."

Eric replied, "I know."

I just looked away into the fire and said nothing more. Of course, he was right, just like Frank would have been right if *he* had said it.

Thank God for Eric. But I wasn't going to say that and risk inflating his ego. I just smirked at him instead.

Heather then walked into the room and said, "I don't mean to interrupt, but I wanted to let you know that I have made up the other guest room for Rudy. He can stay in that guest room, or rather I should say, that can be Rudy's room."

Heather continued, "However, I am here to inform both of you men that we have officially run out of bedrooms in this house, and we should all consider not adding any more children to our brood."

Eric and I both laughed. But she was right. Eric and Heather now had a full house.

Heather added, "I have moved Rudy's suitcases into his room, and I will get him unpacked tomorrow."

I responded, "No, I can do that Heather, but thank you."

She replied, "As you wish, 'most influential person in the community.' And yes, I overheard what Eric said, and everything I heard was totally accurate."

I responded, "Of course it was. That's why he is the smart one. I couldn't even get through college."

Eric sighed and gave me a little slug to the arm. I just laughed.

Heather left the room to give Eric and I our privacy back again.

I looked at Eric and said, "Thank you for taking care of the Rudy situation and making sure he got here."

Eric replied, "It's no problem. And Jonathan and I are becoming friends now, so you better be careful or I might take your job."

I laughed and responded, "Be careful what you wish for. You might still end up with my job, yet."

Eric replied, "I'm just very grateful and happy that you are back HOME. THIS is your HOME. We have all missed you. It's not right when you are gone. That's all I will say before you think that you are more important than you should think you are, even though I just told you that you are."

After a moment, he added, "Oh no! Now I'm starting to sound like you!"

I chuckled and responded, "We all know YOU are the important one here. You are the one running everything. This is home to all of us, and it doesn't run unless *you* are running it."

He replied, "I will assume this is your way of making it clear that you won't be doing the chores with me."

We both laughed, and I responded, "Maybe here and there, only to surprise you on and off."

He replied, "That's fine. Luckily I have a more dependable farmhand who shows up every morning on time."

I responded, "Trevor is an amazing young man. It appears we have both gotten very lucky with kids, without even having kids. Neat magic trick."

We both laughed.

There was a silence as we both looked into the fire. After a couple of moments, I said, "I'm going to find my little man, and get him settled into his room."

Eric responded, "And I am going to bed."

I lifted my tea as a way of toasting him, and he walked out.

I finished the last bit left, brought my mug out into the kitchen, and then made my way upstairs to see if I could track down Rudy.

I found him sitting on his bed in his room. I walked in and sat down next to him. I said, "What are you thinking about?"

He replied, "I'm scared about what is going to happen."

I responded, "I know. I need to get caught up on everything and see how your mom is doing and stuff. But I promise that whatever happens, it will happen with me at your side."

He replied, "I'm scared that something bad happens, and then you go away again, also."

I looked at him intently, and responded, "I am not going away. I promise I will be right here for as long as you need me."

He replied, "You will stay with me? I get to stay with you?"

I responded, "Yep. You are stuck with me."

He smiled and leaned over to hug me. I held him.

Eventually, I said, "I don't want you to worry about what will happen to you. I promise that I will make absolutely certain that you are fine no matter what happens, and I will do it personally, here with you."

I continued, "Just focus on your mom right now. Don't worry about anything else. Okay?"

He nodded his head.

I said, "Do you like this room okay?"

He replied, "I like this room a lot. It feels quiet and safe. Plus, it's not far from your room. I know I will be safe here."

I responded, "Yes, you will be safe here."

After a moment, I said, "Why don't you think about going to bed when you're ready. I am going to be doing the same. We will talk more tomorrow. Okay?"

He replied, "That sounds good, okay. But can I say goodnight to Trevor first?"

I responded, "Absolutely!"

With that, Rudy went to Trevor's room. Trevor was already in bed since he was going to be getting up early to do chores with Eric.

I made my way to my own room. My suitcase had somehow

magically made it into my room without me ever touching it, thanks to Trevor. It felt weird being back in my room. I had so many mixed memories in there. It definitely felt comfortable, like it was MY room. BUT, along with my comfortable and happy memories of being back at the farm, I also had some very dark and sad memories that tried to creep back into my mind. I had experienced some very intense and traumatic moments in that bedroom which still haunted me. I doubt they would ever go away. But I decided to just focus on the comfort of being back home.

The next morning, I woke up really late. YIKES. Jet lag from a three-hour time difference. I dragged myself downstairs, and Heather laughed at me. I laughed also, and said, "Don't even say anything. Yes, I am a lazy soft LA person. I will adjust. Give me time."

Heather replied, "Take your time. Nobody expects anything from you in this house."

Heather had breakfast waiting for me that she had kept in the oven because she likely made it many hours ago when the others had eaten. I had a seat and enjoyed it, while gazing out the dining room window into the beautiful world of the farm that I had missed so much.

Heather came back into the dining room, and said, "Jonathan called for you. He said he had not heard from you. Eric took the call and told him that you had arrived safely and everything was under control."

I replied, "Yeah, I need to talk with him. If you don't mind, I will lock myself in the parlor study and have a talk with him when I'm done eating. I need to speak with him without Rudy being attached to my arm."

Heather responded, "That will be fine. I will tell Rudy and the others that if the door is closed, nobody is to disturb you."

I replied, "Thanks, Heather."

I added, "Speaking of which, where is Rudy?"

Heather responded, "Because you were still sleeping, he went out to the barn with Trevor. They're not making him do chores, but Rudy is keeping Trevor company and helping him with the feed bags and things like that."

I replied, "Okay great. It's good for him."

When I was finished with my breakfast, I brought the dishes out into the kitchen, and then went into the parlor study, while closing the door behind me. I called Jonathan.

Jonathan answered and said, "I was looking for you this morning. I wanted to make sure you were still alive."

I replied, "I wasn't. I was dead to the world. I had a long day yesterday, and then this morning my body thought it was still sitting on a beach in California, apparently."

Jonathan laughed.

I said, "Where are we at with everything?"

He responded, "Well, it sounds quite serious, and even dire, with Rudy's mom. She is in the hospital as we speak. Myself and one of our attorneys went to meet with her just before she left for the hospital. SHE invited US to come over. She was incredibly welcoming, friendly, and very cooperative. She said that Rudy had not stopped talking about you ever since last summer. She informed me that you had made a promise, or offer to her about being there for Rudy in case anything ever happened."

I interjected and said, "Yes, I did. All true."

Jonathan went on, "Well, she was in a serious predicament, and she was scared something might happen to her. She wanted to make sure that Rudy ended up with *you* in case anything happened. Our attorney outlined several options for her to consider, and she agreed to all of our suggestions, just to make sure that Rudy would be taken care of, and that you would have authorization to have him and provide whatever care you saw fit."

Jonathan went on, "I won't go into all of the details right now because you have enough to worry about, but I will just tell you that we have you completely covered legally, regardless of whatever the outcome may be."

I replied, "Thanks, Jonathan. That sounds great."

I added, "What should I be doing now? Anything?"

He responded, "Nothing. In fact, Rudy's mom doesn't really want him to see her at the hospital in her current condition. She feels it would scare and traumatize him. She prefers that he think of her as she was before being admitted, and that if she is feeling better after the treatments, he can come see her at that time."

I replied, "Okay. Hmmm. I am just wondering how long this goes on for. Like, should I enroll him in school here? Or just wait? Or?"

Jonathan responded, "Between you and I, it doesn't look good. Speaking as your friend only, if it were me, I would enroll him in school and get him into a solid stable routine. Even if things work out well in the end, it looks like this is going to go on for two months or more."

I replied, "Oh, I see."

He responded, "Are you okay with all of this?"

I replied, "Yeah, with Rudy, yeah. I'm just unsettled by what could happen to *her* and how Rudy will take it. But yeah, I have no doubts about taking care of Rudy. None at all."

Jonathan responded, "Yeah I understand."

I then said, "I know you probably have regular business for me also. I am going to come see you in town, but Thanksgiving is in a few days, and I am trying to get settled in. How about if we meet at the Carlisle house after Thanksgiving? Is that okay?"

He replied, "Yeah, that sounds great. Take your time. There is nothing pressing. But yes, I need to talk with you about a few items."

I responded, "Okay, I will let you know when. In the meantime, let me know if anything happens, or if you need anything from me."

He replied, "Yeah, we are in touch with the hospital, and in fact, we have authorization to receive medical updates. I will let you know if I hear anything. And welcome back. Welcome HOME. We are delighted to have you back where you belong."

I chuckled and responded, "Yeah, thank you. And I know. Sorry I was away. But I'm here now, and I'm glad to be back home, also."

I ended my call with Jonathan. I went back out into the kitchen to find Heather. She was there, and I said, "Heather, I may need your help. I'm kind of lost when it comes to taking care of kids, and school, and things like that. Jonathan is telling me that I might need to enroll Rudy in school here. I have no clue."

Heather smiled and replied, "It's no problem. I just went through all of that with Trevor, and I can take care of that with Rudy."

She went on, "A few of us parents have an entire carpool system worked out. We each drive a few of the kids into town for school a couple of times a week. Sometimes I only have to do it once. It works really well. I can add Rudy to the equation."

I responded, "Oh, wow that's great. So, I guess I don't have to go and hire a limo service to bring Rudy to and from school every day?"

Heather started laughing at me. I realized that what I had just said likely sounded very weird and ostentatious. I was embarrassed. I think I even turned red.

Heather, through her laughter replied, "No, we will all work it out. The parents out here all work together."

I responded, "Well as you can tell, I'm clueless. I will need you to walk me through every little thing, I'm afraid. I wasn't expecting to have a kid in school."

She replied, "Yes, I totally know how you feel."

I responded, "Okay. Well, I know the kids are probably off from school for Thanksgiving. Let's see what happens with Rudy's mom, and then maybe we will proceed with enrolling Rudy into school the week after Thanksgiving?"

Heather replied, "That sounds like a reasonable plan."

I gave Heather a wave and went outside to see what Eric and the boys were up to.

When I stumbled into the barn, Eric looked at me and said, "Good lord, have you been sleeping all day? The day is almost over. You are a lazy city slicker now."

I replied, "Yes, I know. It's pathetic. Believe me, I have felt pathetic all day. Don't worry, I will adjust, Boss."

Eric laughed and responded, "Well, we have everything under control here, so take your time."

I kept looking around for Rudy. I spotted him sweeping in the barn. I found that amusing and had a good chuckle over that.

I asked, "You doing okay?"

He replied, "Yeah, things are fine now that you're back home."

I went over closer to him and responded, "I wanted to make sure that you understood what the plans were for this whole situation."

He looked at me, anxiously waiting.

I said, "Your mom is currently in the hospital getting her treatments so that she can get better. It might take a while for her to get better. Therefore, I think it would be a good idea for you to start school here. You would be going into town with Trevor, and to his school. How do you feel about that?"

Rudy replied, "Yeah, Trevor already told me about his school, and he wants me to go with him. Trevor said he will introduce me to his friends, and that they are nice. I am okay going to that school if you decide that is what I need."

I responded, "Okay, good. We will have Thanksgiving coming up here, and then after the holiday, Heather is going to work on getting you into school the week after that. Okay?"

He replied, "Okay, that is fine."

Then he said, "Will you be leaving to go anywhere anytime soon? Because I'm afraid you will leave, and I won't know where you went."

I smiled and responded, "I won't go anywhere without telling you first; and I have no plans to leave this farm until after Thanksgiving. Okay?"

He smiled and nodded.

Thanksgiving was coming in a few days, and I was finally settled back into the farm. I was going to bed earlier, and waking up earlier. I was seeing the sunrises, and watching the sunsets. I felt that I was finally back into the rhythm of life. I found myself noticing constant reminders of Frank everywhere.

Although Eric and Heather had made the farmhouse their own, they left most things alone. This gave me comfort, and it showed me that they had a respect for Frank, and perhaps also for me in regard to my desire to keep those reminders of Frank alone.

By far, my most favorite room to hang out in was the living room. That is where Frank and I had most of our talks, and that is where Eric and Heather had left alone many of his mementoes that I had not packed up.

I had already told Eric that I was going to take all of the mementoes to Mr. Wilkens' house when it was finished. So, I made it clear that I was wanting all of that stuff for myself, but I didn't want to pack it up until I could see it all on display in my new home. I felt it was very considerate of Eric and Heather to just leave all of that in the living room untouched until I decided to pack it up myself.

I enjoyed sitting in the living room with the fire going, and looking at all of Frank's stuff. I think for the most part, Eric, Heather, and Trevor, considered the living room to be 'my room,' and I had plenty of peace and quiet in there. Conversely, I stayed out of the kitchen, which I considered to be 'their room,' along with the dining room when we were not eating together. I think it worked out well. I had feared that I was intruding upon Eric and Heather's home life, but honestly, it seemed that all of us were cohabitating very efficiently.

With that said, it occurred to me that Rudy and I were most surely driving their grocery expense through the roof. Yes, much of our food came from the farm itself, but Heather still did a weekly shopping in town as Frank had done, and their grocery bill must have more than doubled. Plus, Thanksgiving was coming, and that was going to be costly, I am sure.

I decided to fix that. I walked into the kitchen and handed Heather a check. I told her it was for food, and especially since Thanksgiving was upon us. She looked at the check, ripped it up into several pieces, and then handed it back to me with a smile.

I just sighed. I smiled, and said, "We will settle this a different way."

She laughed.

It might take me a bit, but I was determined to figure out a way to make my contribution. I just needed to figure it out, and I was sure that I eventually would.

It was the night before Thanksgiving, and I was excited to enjoy Thanksgiving at the farm. I was excited mostly for the feast. I had originally expected to still be in LA for Thanksgiving, and I felt fortunate to be at the farm instead. I had called my mom and informed her of my entire situation, and that I had dropped out of college, come back home, was taking care of Rudy, and that I was going to be having Thanksgiving at the farm. I told her that I would stop by and see her when I went into town for my meeting with Jonathan.

As always, my mom was overwhelmed with all of the information I had thrown at her all at once, and she didn't know what to say. She only replied that she had bought a new bird feeder, and that they were going to have a quiet Thanksgiving, her and my stepfather, at home.

As with all holidays, I had planned on helping Eric with the chores so that they would be done quickly and easily. I woke up early Thanksgiving morning to go out and help Eric and Trevor. I was going to let Rudy come out when he was ready. Rudy would come out and help, but 8:00AM was more his speed. I could have asked him to be out there at 4:00AM like the rest of us, but his mom was deathly ill in the hospital, and I didn't think I needed to over stress him with slave labor on top of everything else. Eric and Trevor were equally understanding and had no issues with Rudy joining in late after he woke up.

I wasn't outside for more than a half an hour when Heather came outside yelling for me. She said it was Jonathan, and it was urgent. Welcome to my life. I ran inside and took the call. Jonathan had some stunning news that would change everyone's lives forever, especially Rudy's.

Jonathan had received a call from the hospital informing him that Rudy's mom had passed away. The news sent a chill up and down my spine. My mind froze up. The brain error message was caused by the converging issues of having to tell Rudy that his mom had died, along with the other issue of me now being the permanent caregiver for Rudy. Both of those items were a bit overwhelming to digest.

After the news, I told Jonathan I would call him later. I went into the kitchen and told Heather. She didn't know what to say. I then went out into the barn and discreetly whispered the news to Eric.

Eric stopped what he was doing, and responded, "What should we do?"

I replied, "Nothing. You guys keep doing what you are doing. I need to speak with Rudy, and we will go from there."

I went back inside, and sat down by the fireplace for a few moments to think. I realized that I already had felt that Rudy was my child, and honestly, I didn't feel much differently then, from how I felt the day before. I decided that from my end of things, there was nothing to freak out about. So, the only huge issue was having to break the news to Rudy. How do you tell a child that his mother has died?

It occurred to me that Eric had already done a similar task, by telling Trevor that his dad had died. Eric was way ahead of me. I remember how Eric did it, by being very straightforward and honest. I decided that how Eric did it must be the correct way, because Eric usually did things the correct way.

I decided to go upstairs and see if Rudy was awake yet. I got to his room, peeked inside, and he looked over at me. He was awake, but still in bed. I went inside and sat down on his bed. He looked at me solemnly, and his eyes were a bit red.

I said, "I have something I need to tell you, Rudy."

He replied, "I already know."

His eyes were turning even more red, but he wasn't crying. His solemn look made me think that maybe he really did know. But how could he possibly know??

I just stared at him, wondering if he was referring to something else, or what was going on, exactly. Perhaps I still needed to tell him?

When I was about to say something else, Rudy said, "I know it's my mom. I know she's not here anymore."

I was in shock that he knew, and had said that. I decided to reach down and sort of give him a hug, as much as you can do with someone laying in bed. I then sat back up and just looked at him in silence.

After a few moments I said, "I'm sorry, Son."

When I said that, he started crying a little bit, but softly.

I was way too curious to let it go, so I asked, "How did you know, Son?"

He rubbed his eyes, and replied, "My mom visited me right before I woke up."

I just kept staring at him, trying to process and understand what he was saying.

He continued, "She came to me in my dream. I saw her. I knew it was her. I knew it was real. She said that she had to go, but that she loved me and that she would always stay with me, inside."

I just stared at him. What does a person say to something like that?

He went on, "I am okay. I'm okay because she came to see me. I feel her with me. I know it's okay."

He sat up in bed and I hugged him. My eyes were a bit red. I couldn't believe his strength, disposition, and attitude. I was in disbelief about his story of the dream, but I also knew he was telling the truth. I knew what he had described was real and happened.

I noticed standing outside Rudy's bedroom in the hallway, were Eric and Heather. I motioned for them to come in. They both took turns hugging Rudy and saying they were sorry. At that moment, I realized I should do something. I told everyone I would be right back, and I motioned for Heather and Eric to stay there with Rudy.

I went downstairs, and outside to the barn looking for Trevor. I found him working.

I said, "Trevor, do you remember when you and I had that man-to-man talk last summer?"

He replied, "Yes."

I responded, "I want to have another one with you now."

He replied, "Okay."

I responded, "Trevor, I wanted to tell you myself that Rudy's mom just passed away this morning."

Trevor's head sunk down.

He replied, "I bet Rudy is very sad."

I responded, "Yes, he is."

Then I said, "Trevor, I would like to ask you a favor, man-to-man."

I continued, "You have already gone through this. I was hoping you could talk to Rudy, and maybe help him as best you can."

Trevor replied, "Yes, Sir. I can do that. I want to help Rudy. I understand how he feels. I know what it's like. I will help him."

I responded, "Thank you, Trevor, I knew I could count on you."

He replied, "Yes you can, Sir."

Trevor followed me back inside the farmhouse. We both went upstairs. Eric and Heather were comforting Rudy. Trevor walked inside Rudy's room. Rudy saw him and seemed very interested and happy that Trevor was there.

I motioned for Eric and Heather to come out into the hallway with me. I left Trevor in the room alone with Rudy. I saw Trevor rubbing Rudy on the shoulder and saying that he understood what it's like.

Now, some people, some parents, might think this is weird, or that I did the wrong thing, here. But I decided to leave the two boys alone. I motioned for Eric and Heather to come downstairs with me. Something deep inside told me that this was the correct thing to do, however unorthodox it might be to leave one child in charge of comforting another child after the death of a parent.

I thought I would leave them alone for half an hour, and then I would go back up.

About twenty-five minutes later, Trevor and Rudy came walking downstairs and into the living room together. All of us were surprised. Rudy seemed very calm and doing okay.

I motioned for Rudy to come over to me so I could give him a hug. I whispered in his ear, "Are you doing okay, Son?"

He replied so that everyone could hear, "I am sad, but I'm okay. Trevor understands me, and it makes it better."

I looked over at Trevor and gave him a smile and a 'thumbs up.'

Heather went over to Trevor and gave him an approving rub on his shoulders and stroked his hair with her hand, while smiling.

Eric and Heather started leaving the room, and they herded Trevor out with them. Once Rudy and I were alone, I said, "I don't really know how best to help you. You need to tell me what you want and need."

Rudy thought for a moment and replied, "I just want to know what will happen to me now."

I looked into his eyes and responded, "You will stay with me now."

He replied, "Always? Or just for a little while?"

I responded, "For the rest of my life."

He looked like he was going to cry, and he sunk into my arms. I held him for as long as he wanted.

When he let go, he said, "I'm going to be sad for a long time. But as long as I am with you, and I am staying with you, I will be okay."

I hugged him again.

After a while, I asked, "What do you want to do today? Do you need to be alone, or just with me, or in your room, or outside, or what would you like to do?"

He thought for a moment, and replied, "Today is Thanksgiving. I want to have Thanksgiving. Trevor said Heather is making a huge dinner."

I responded, "Okay. But if you feel sad, or you need me in private, just tug on my arm and we can go talk, okay?"

He nodded his head in acknowledgement.

I walked him into the kitchen where the others were standing together.

I said, "Rudy wants to have Thanksgiving."

Heather responded, "Then Thanksgiving is what we will have."

Thereafter, Rudy stayed close to either me or Trevor. He didn't seem to want to be alone. Also, as long as he was with me or Trevor, he seemed to do really well, considering the circumstances.

When it came time for our feast, we all took our seats. Eric looked at me to do our meal prayer. I looked at everyone, and said, "God bless Rudy's mother. Let us all be thankful for each other, and that we are all together. While we have much to be sad about, we have even more to be thankful for. Let us all remember that always. We all belong here!"

All of us heard Rudy say, "God bless my mom."

And that was it. Then we started eating.

While the mood was not jovial, it was calm and peaceful. Maybe even pleasant.

At no time did Rudy have any kind of emotional meltdown (as I would have had in his position). He was very subdued and sad, but he remained very calm and together. I decided to just let things flow and not keep bringing the subject up, as long as he was doing so well.

I decided to leave Jonathan alone for the rest of Thanksgiving. Mrs. Carlisle would have disapproved of me bothering anyone on Thanksgiving.

However, the next morning I called Jonathan.

I said, "Can you give me the specifics of my legal situation regarding Rudy?"

Jonathan replied, "Rudy's mom was amazingly cooperative with us when we met her. She genuinely and truly wanted you to have Rudy. She even mentioned that if she survived her illness, she still wanted you listed as the person in her will to get custody in the event she passed away for a different reason later on. Thus, we have a couple of different documents from her."

He continued, "We have an agreement that gives you full custody in the case of her death due to this illness. But even more than that, we have her Last Will and Testament, giving you full custody in the case of her death, by any instance. And not only that, but she listed YOU as the Executor of her will so that you have full control of the process."

I responded, "Wow. You are amazing Jonathan. This is why I knew to just trust that you would do the right things."

Jonathan replied, "However sad this all is, you can be assured that you have custody locked in. I will file with the court for a formal permanent custody order. It won't be any problem considering all of the documents we have."

I responded, "Thank you. That's great."

After a pause, I said, "Is there any other family involved; or do we need to take care of her apartment and everything else?"

He replied, "There is nobody of note. That is why she didn't know what to do with Rudy. She has family, but she has very little to do with them."

I responded, "Okay. Well, let's take great care to clean out her apartment and keep EVERYTHING of any sentimental value for Rudy. Then make sure all of her rent and utility bills are cleared and settled. Also, let's make sure she is cremated and that we get the ashes. I will pay for everything personally."

Jonathan replied, "Yes, Sir."

I responded, "Let's get through the weekend in one piece hopefully. Then how about I come into town and see you on Monday?"

He replied, "Sounds great. See you then."

We had a pretty quiet rest of the holiday weekend. Rudy was really silent and down, but he was fully functional and doing okay. Trevor was doing a great job at keeping him occupied and his mind off of things.

I sat down and had some tea with Eric and Heather at the dining room table when the boys were talking amongst themselves upstairs.

I said, "Guys, I'm going to need your help."

Heather spoke up, and replied, "Anything at all; we are always here for you."

I responded, "I have a Carlisle Trust meeting in town on Monday. I am not sure if Rudy will insist on coming or not. You would think he would stay here after losing his mom, but from what I know of Rudy, it won't shock me if he wants to come with me. I've decided to do whatever he wants to do."

I continued, "But he needs to get enrolled in school. I was wondering if you can help me with that, Heather?"

She replied, "Yes. I will agree to do the carpool on Monday, and will go into the school and take care of everything that's needed. Quite frankly, once they find out who Rudy's foster parent is, I doubt there will be any obstacles from anyone."

I responded, "Great, thank you so much. I just can't cope with all of that on top of everything else."

I continued, "I am thinking it would be great if Rudy starts school on Friday as kind of an easy gradual way in. Then he can contemplate over the weekend, and be more comfortable jumping fully into it on Monday."

Heather replied, "That sounds reasonable to me. I will talk to the school and get it all set up."

I responded, "Perfect. Thank God for you guys."

Eric quipped, "No, that's our line to you."

I responded, "I guess this family has turned into a mutual appreciation society."

We chuckled.

Then I had a final thought, and said, "I will have Jonathan get all of Rudy's legal papers and health records for you, Heather."

She replied, "Yes, I will need those."

I responded, "I will have someone from the office meet you at the school with everything."

She replied, "That will work."

When Sunday night arrived, I thought I should mention my upcoming meeting in town with Jonathan to Rudy, so that he wouldn't freak out Monday morning.

He came into the living room to sit with me, and I said, "I want to let you know that I have to go into town tomorrow for a meeting at The Carlisle Trust, and .."

I didn't even get to finish my sentence. He interjected, "I'm going with you."

I smiled amusingly, and responded, "Yeah, I figured as much. I just didn't know if you would be in the mood for a serious business meeting. Are you sure?"

He replied, "I'm going wherever you go."

Reminding myself that I was not going to oppose him on this issue for a while, I responded, "Yep, okay."

But then I added, "You are starting school on Friday with Trevor. Then it will be regular after that, starting the following Monday."

I sort of feared that he might freak out or show resistance to that. But he surprised me by saying, "Good. I am ready for school again, and going with Trevor makes it not scary."

I responded, "Perfect. I'm very proud of how you are handling everything, Son."

He smiled at me with pride.

On Monday, Heather was off with Trevor and the rest of the kids in the carpool. Eric was busy working in the barn. Rudy and I were getting ready for our own mission that day. After we had eaten and gotten ready, Rudy and I headed off in the truck into town to the Carlisle house for 'our' meeting.

We went inside the house, and Jonathan came running down the stairs to greet us. He had a big smile on his face of excitement. But once he saw Rudy, he toned it down to a more solemn tone.

He looked at Rudy and said, "I am so sorry, Rudy, about your mom."

Rudy replied, "Yes, thank you, Sir."

Jonathan looked at me, as if wanting guidance on how to act, or what to do. I had not warned him that Rudy was coming. I just didn't think of it. I knew Jonathan was likely wondering how sad or delicate Rudy was, and if this would affect what we discussed, or how we discussed it.

I said, "It was a rough couple of days, but Rudy has been doing great. I have been very proud of how he is handling himself. He is very brave and very strong. He wanted to come to this meeting today because he is ready to help with our missions."

I was hoping that would make Rudy feel good, but also signal to Jonathan that he could speak freely and not worry about Rudy being too fragile.

Jonathan took the signal and resumed his excited mood that he had when we came through the door.

He said, "It's not all done yet, but I'm excited to show you what we have done with the offices upstairs."

I replied, "Oh, are you all moved in up there already?"

He responded, "Yeah, pretty much. Come see."

Rudy and I followed him upstairs. It looked all finished to me. He had kept the original wood floors, but refinished them to a really light and shiny finish, different from the previous dark finish that Mrs. Carlisle had. He had removed the intricate floral wallpaper (cough) that Mrs. Carlisle had in the hallway, and instead, painted the walls a calming light gray. He kept all of the very bold and classy wood trim, and painted that white with some green accents here and there. It looked great!

He showed me the offices, in which some of them had Carlisle Trust officers working. I was not looking for long introductions to everyone, so I just poked my head in and waved to them. But once they saw Rudy, there were various comments about how "cute" and "dear" he looked. Jonathan sensed I was just wanting a low-key quick visit, so he kept it moving along. However, it occurred to me that I really needed to come back sometime for the purpose of meeting the staff and taking some time to speak with them all.

We finally got to what he called "the boardroom," translated as "the conference room," or "meeting room." I walked inside. It was fantastic! I could see that this was surely what he was excited to show me. It felt very much like Mrs. Carlisle's parlor room downstairs where she held all of *her* Carlisle Trust meetings. Jonathan had cleverly continued that feeling and mood upstairs in this room. Best of all was the fact it had an amazing view of the park. Jonathan saw me notice it right away, and he was beaming from ear to ear. He knew I would love this, and I did!

I exclaimed, "THIS IS FANTASTIC, JONATHAN! I can't think of a better place to have meetings than in this house, while looking out at the park."

He replied, "I know. I was so excited when I realized it, and I hoped you would be as delighted as me."

I responded, "Indeed! Well done!"

But then I said, "However, I am wondering why this is not YOUR office? You're here all of the time, and you deserve this view."

He replied, "There was another room I wanted more."

I responded, "REALLY? What room is better than this?"

He replied, "It's not better. It's more meaningful."

He started walking out of the boardroom, presumably to show me his office. I followed, and Rudy followed me, as he remained silent. Jonathan led us into his personal office. It was a normal looking office, although pleasant. I was not sure what about it made it so appealing, though.

I said, "So, what about your office makes it so meaningful to you?"

He replied, "When I was just out of high school and had recently started working for Mrs. Carlisle, I was going through some personal issues that were very difficult for me. I was pretty much having a total breakdown, without going into details. Mrs. Carlisle asked me to have dinner with her here at her home. We had long talks, and she showed so much kindness to me that evening. She asked me to spend the night at her home, and offered me a guest bedroom up here. My conversations with her that night changed my life and made me feel better. And this room we are currently standing in, my new office, is the exact guest bedroom that I stayed in that night. It's meaningful because the night I spent in this guest bedroom made me feel so much better about my life. It healed me. So, I am delighted to now have my office in this room."

I quipped, "Wow! And wow!"

I continued, "Wow, because now I understand why this room means so much to you. But wow again, because I find it remarkable that both of us had similar experiences with Mrs. Carlisle changing our lives with her time, attention, and words. I had a very similar visit with Mrs. Carlisle that changed EVERYTHING for me."

I added, "It's hard to imagine how many lives she touched and deeply affected. Nobody will ever do that again. The Carlisle's were epic."

Jonathan replied, "Agreed. But I need YOU to try and match that."

We both chuckled.

Jonathan walked us back over to the meeting room. He was quick to take his seat at the table, so that my seat would be the one to have the perfect view of the park. Rudy then also took a seat. I gave Jonathan my full attention so that he would start.

He said, "There is a lot going on, but I want to focus on two things today. First, we have had the new behavioral counselor at the high school for two months now, and Mr. Bowman reports that incidents requiring discipline have decreased by half."

I replied, "That is fantastic. I knew that would help."

He responded, "Yes, and even Mr. Bowman seemed surprised and grateful by the initial results."

I replied, "Good. Maybe he will come around eventually. But I want to continue being aggressive with this program. I want to go from a 50% decrease, and bring it as close to no incidents as possible. We still have work to do."

Jonathan responded, "Yes, Sir. But so far, so good."

I replied, "Let's watch it, and I might consider adding a second counselor."

He responded, "Yeah, I knew you would say that. We will check in on this again after a few more months of results."

I replied, "Sounds good."

After a pause, Jonathan said, "The second item is something I want to raise so that you can give it some thought for next time."

I replied, "Okay. What do you got for me?"

He responded, "We still need to spend more money before the end of the year, and Christmas is coming. You need to give me some direction of what you might want to do, perhaps involving Christmas."

I looked at Rudy, then back at Jonathan. I thought for a moment.

I said, "Obviously, I think we will end up doing some kind of a major donation or giveaway of some sort. But secondly, I think we should do something special for the community, *involving* the community."

Jonathan was listening intently.

I continued, "Maybe we should have a community Christmas party or festival of some sort. We could have it right here at the park."

I looked over at Rudy and said, "What do you think of that idea, Rudy?"

Rudy looked surprised that I was including him in the conversation; but he saw that even Jonathan was now looking at him, and wondering what his response might be.

Rudy thought for a moment, and replied, "Whatever you do, make it fun for kids. Don't just do something boring for adults."

Jonathan and I laughed.

Jonathan responded, "You are absolutely right, Rudy."

Then Jonathan looked at me and said, "This idea has potential. Let's all think about it and discuss it more next time."

He then looked at Rudy and said, "Young man, maybe you can think of some ideas we should consider that kids your age, younger, and older, might enjoy doing?"

Rudy replied, "Yes, Sir. I can do that, Sir."

I couldn't help but get a smug proud smirk on my face, as Jonathan chuckled and said, "Perfect. Thank you."

Jonathan looked at me and said, "Maybe we meet again in a week or so?"

I replied, "Sounds good. See you then."

I added, "Now that the offices are done and I know your office is up here, we can just let ourselves out, and we'll know where to find you when we arrive from now on."

Jonathan responded, "Okay, cool."

Rudy and I waved to him and left.

When we got outside, Rudy said, "Can we go sit on the bench before we go back home?"

I replied, "Great idea, but I have something more interesting for today."

He responded, "What could be more interesting than sitting on that magical bench?"

I chuckled and replied, "Well, nothing is more magical than sitting on the bench. BUT, what might be more interesting is that I was thinking of taking you to the house I grew up in and having you meet my parents."

He responded, "They live here?"

I replied, "Yes, just up the street. That's why I spent my childhood at the park."

He responded, "Wow. Yes, okay."

I was debating whether to walk or drive, but I knew if we walked, it would turn into a much longer event, because I would end up stopping at Mr. Wilkens' house and telling him long stories. Thus, I decided for this visit we would just focus on my parents, and should drive up the street directly to their house.

The strangest and most surreal thing was that I still had my bedroom at my parent's house. It was a situation where I had "gone off to college," so I still kept my bedroom there with all of my stuff in it. It seemed ridiculous at this point because I felt VERY OLD, was no longer in college, and there was NO WAY I was ever going to be staying at my parent's house again. Yet, it was still there with all of my stuff still inside it, as if I was 10 or 16 years old. Weird.

This made me realize that I should really pack up all of my things and give my parents their space. I could just move all of my personal things to the Wilkens house and store it there. Add another task to my growing list of things that needed to be done.

We drove down the street and parked at my parent's house. I had called my mother earlier to warn her that we might stop by, and to see if she had any interest in meeting Rudy. She seemed excited at the prospect, so she would be expecting us.

We walked up to the front door, and I knocked on the door. How weird is that? I was still kind of living there, in the sense that my bedroom was still there, and I had a key, but it still felt so wrong to just walk right in without knocking.

My mom answered the door. She looked at me with a pleasant smile, gave me a hug; but then switched her entire focus to Rudy, where it remained for the rest of our visit. She was super nice with Rudy; very inviting, soft, kind, animated, conversational, patient, gentle, and I was wondering where my real mom had gone. Then I realized that my real mom was likely stuffed in one of the closets somewhere, and replacing her was a GRANDMOTHER. Grandmothers are COMPLETELY DIFFERENT from moms, for those who didn't know.

My stepfather tore himself away from whatever he was doing, and walked into the kitchen to join us. He gave me a little grunt and a wave, and then gave Rudy his full attention. My mom introduced Rudy to him. He looked like he was inspecting Rudy. He observed him, and looked him over for a few seconds, and then gave out a little cough. I suppose my stepfather might have thought that Rudy seemed a bit too much like me? But with that said, he ended up being really nice and kind to Rudy after that. It was a bizarre experience for me, overall.

I said to Rudy, "Do you want to see my old bedroom?"

He replied, "YEAH!"

My stepfather piped up and said, "Yeah, it's still your bedroom. All your stuff is still there. Now that you are Mr. Big Bucks, we should be charging you rent."

Nice guy, my stepfather always was.

I replied, "Yes, true. But consider this my 'notice to vacate.' I'm going to move it all down to Mr. Wilkens' house so that you guys can have that room back as a guest room or whatever you want."

My mom responded, "Are you moving to Mr. Wilkens' house?"

I replied, "Not anytime soon, but it's going to be one of my homes, yes."

My stepfather jumped back in and said, "One of your many

dozens of homes all over the world?"

I looked at my mom. But my stepfather wasn't done. He added, "Maybe you can pay back what we had to give you to fix your car out in California."

I sighed, and replied, "Sure. I'll have my attorneys get in touch with you to settle things up."

Of course, I WAS KIDDING! JOKING! My mom looked at me in a huff because she thought I was trying to start a fight. I WASN'T! I was kidding. Ugh.

I made a mental note that there would not be any further visits until Christmas Eve. Just too prickly!

I smiled and started leading Rudy upstairs to my room. We went into my room, and he looked all around, as if he was video recording everything with his eyes for later viewing. It sort of reminded me of how I had acted in Mr. Wilkens' house when I was Rudy's age.

I also looked all around my room. It was weird. I had been in there last year on Christmas Eve, but it seemed more like ten years had passed. I took notice of the games Mr. Wilkens had given me. I definitely wanted those, along with the pinecone Mrs. Carlisle had given me. In a way, my stepfather was right, and I had delayed way too long clearing out my room. Perhaps I had been inconsiderate by keeping all of my things in their house. I decided to chill-out, and seriously take care of clearing things out of my parent's house. Plus, I would need to pay my stepfather back now that I had money. No need for hard feelings. My bad.

I let Rudy have a good long look, but then I decided it might be best for us to make a very friendly, smooth, kind exit, and get back to the farm. I herded Rudy back downstairs. I told my mom that we needed to get back home. She asked when we could stop by again.

I said, "We will definitely be here for Christmas Eve like always."

She seemed a bit disappointed by my answer, but quickly covered it up, and started telling Rudy how delightful it was to meet him, and that she couldn't wait to see him again.

Even my stepfather walked back into the room and told Rudy that he was looking forward to seeing him again (I felt he was being truly sincere). I gave my stepfather a friendly wave, and we walked to the door, and my mom saw us out.

She said, "Please don't be a stranger."

She added, "Next time you come over, Rudy, we can make cookies, or anything you like to do."

Rudy replied, "OKAY!"

We waved and left. Rudy and I climbed back into the truck and left for the farm.

After a few moments, I said, "So what did you think of *THAT*?"

I couldn't help but laugh.

Rudy responded, "Your mom is really nice. But your stepfather seems to like me more than he likes you."

I laughed and laughed. Perfectly said. No comment from me needed.

But then I said, "Yeah, they did seem to like you quite a bit. It's nice."

I added, "Let's see how the visit goes on Christmas Eve."

Rudy responded, "Yeah, Okay."

We arrived back at the farm, and I went into the kitchen to greet Eric and Heather.

Eric said, "How did all of that go today?"

I replied, "The meeting with Jonathan was fine. Rudy was great. But then we went to my parents so that I could let them meet Rudy."

Eric and Heather gave me a look of amusement like they were thinking of making popcorn first before hearing the rest of the story.

Eric smirked and said, "And how was *THAT*?"

I replied, "Charming as ever."

They both laughed.

Then I added, "They were super nice to Rudy. Even my

stepfather was very kind to him. My mother seems to absolutely adore him."

Heather responded, "Well that's nice at least."

I replied, "Yeah. We should be able to endure Christmas Eve there okay. They have to behave to a certain degree with Rudy there."

Eric responded, "If you guys are definitely going to your parents for Christmas Eve, then I think the three of us will go to my mom's for Christmas Eve."

I replied, "Sounds like a plan. Then we can all meet back at the farm before bedtime?"

Eric responded, "Yep."

I gave him a 'thumbs up.'

Tuesday morning came, and I realized that I had forgotten to ask Heather how the school enrollment for Rudy went. I scooted into the kitchen and inquired. Heather informed me that everything went perfectly fine, and that they were expecting Rudy to start on Friday.

She further explained that one of the ladies in the school administrative office had actually known Rudy's mom, and therefore was very sensitive to the situation. I thanked Heather for taking care of all that for me.

However, Rudy didn't want to wait until Friday. On Wednesday night, Rudy came up to me and asked if he could start school a day early.

I replied, "Why do you want to start early? You don't need to start until Friday."

He responded, "Trevor told me that they're learning about frogs in science class tomorrow, and will have real frogs. I don't want to miss that. So, can I go tomorrow instead of Friday?"

I didn't have an answer to that. I told him to wait at the fireplace while I went into the kitchen to speak with Heather. Fortunately, I caught Heather before she was going upstairs to bed. I explained to her what Rudy had just said. I asked her if she thought Rudy could go tomorrow, or if we needed to wait until Friday.

Heather responded, "He can go tomorrow. I am doing carpool tomorrow. Plus, the school told me that he could start whenever you were ready for him to start. Like I said before, once they found out that it was you fostering him, they pretty much said we could do whatever you decided was best."

I replied, "Well if you have a child Rudy's age who is begging to go to school, I view that as a lucky signal to send him."

Heather laughed, and responded, "I agree."

Heather and I discussed what time Rudy had to be ready, and I told her that I would make sure he was ready. I wished her a goodnight.

I went back into the living room and told Rudy that he could go to school the next morning, but that he had to be ready to leave at the set time, and not be even five minutes late. He seemed excited and said he would set his alarm. Then he said something amusing.

He said, "But make sure you are not in the bathroom when I need it, because now I am on a schedule."

He was right. While Eric and Heather had their own bathroom in the large bedroom, me and the two boys were sharing the other bathroom that was upstairs. There was a half-bath downstairs, but no shower in that one.

I said to Rudy, "I will let you two boys have the bathroom. I'll use the bathroom after you guys leave for school."

He replied, "Yeah, that will work. Okay."

I chuckled and then went into his bedroom to make sure his alarm clock was set correctly. I wished him a goodnight.

I went into my own bedroom and made sure that my alarm clock was set. I wanted to make sure he got up and was on time for Heather on his first day.

Morning came, and Rudy was up and doing as he was supposed to be doing, and on schedule. I waited for him downstairs. He came downstairs, clean, all dressed, and looking ready for his first day. He had breakfast, and it was time for them to go.

I found myself getting a little choked up at the sight of my little man heading off for his first day of school under my parentage.

Heather took a picture of Rudy and Trevor together, as a way to commemorate Rudy's first day.

I looked at him, smiled, gave him a big hug, and said, "I am so proud of you, Rudy."

I added, "Have a nice day and I will see you later."

Rudy smiled and waved as he walked out.

I sat at the dining room table, completely alone, and contemplated all that had recently happened. I had returned to California, returned to college, returned to dropping out again, then I returned back home, returned back to my job, returned to my true reality, and now Rudy had returned back to school. But what struck me the most was that I truly felt that I had returned to living a meaningful life.

CHAPTER TWO
The Christmas

The cool and crisp Fall days of autumn leaves gave way to the distinct chill of Winter, and the smell of balsam pines and cinnamon spice. Christmas season was upon us.

It was time to meet with Jonathan at The Carlisle Trust to discuss my plans for Christmas. Since Rudy had been involved in the previous discussion regarding the idea of a community Christmas celebration, I decided that I wanted to include him in this follow-up meeting as well. For that reason, I scheduled my meeting with Jonathan to take place right after Rudy would be getting out of school. I would go pick him up at school, and then we would go to The Carlisle Trust meeting together.

As I waited in the truck outside the school, I could see Rudy walking over with a smile of excitement on his face. I'm willing to guess that he was the only boy of his age excited to go to a business meeting. Yet, somehow, he was. He loved the fact that I was including him in my meetings with The Carlisle Trust. Although he was always silent, he never seemed bored. He thrived on listening and understanding everything that Jonathan and I would be discussing.

However, at our previous meeting, Jonathan and I had changed the equation by directly asking for Rudy's input. Now that Rudy felt his opinion was desired and of value, there was no holding him back. He seemed to want to be more involved and interactive with our discussions.

Some parents might disagree with my approach and willingness to allow a child to have involvement in serious adult business discussions; but this was what Rudy wanted, and I believed in teaching kids as early as they were willing to learn. After all, I was not much older than Rudy when Frank made me a 'camp leader;' and I wasn't even old enough for my driver's license when I took over full operational control of The Lake resort after Benny's heart attack. In my family, we start them young.

Anyway, Rudy and I scooted over from his school to The Carlisle Trust office at the Carlisle house. We went right upstairs to Jonathan's office. We all greeted each other, and then headed into the meeting room.

We each took our customary seats, and Jonathan started the meeting by saying, "So Rudy, how is school going?"

Rudy replied, "It's good. I like school here. Trevor is in my class so it makes it good."

Jonathan responded, "Well I'm glad you've joined us for the meeting today. We might need your ideas."

Rudy smiled with glee.

Jonathan gave a pause, and then looked at me and said, "Have you given any thought to what you want to do for Christmas?"

I replied, "Yes, I know what I want to do. Well, actually I want to do a few things. But as far as our big expenditure, I know what I want to do."

Jonathan stared at me, waiting for my announcement. I hesitated on purpose as a way of building suspense.

Then I said, "I want to fill some semi-trucks full of toys for kids of all ages. Then we pull them up alongside the park, and we give away everything inside them to everyone in the community who feels they need them."

Rudy's eyes popped open. Jonathan scratched his head, moved around in his chair, and then gave me a smile like he loved it, but also a look as if he thought I was being crazy and unrealistic. I just stared at him in a dead-serious calm way.

Jonathan changed his facial expressions a few more times, and then replied, "That is the most simple, obvious, crazy, complicated, logical, difficult, and brilliant idea."

I responded, "Yeah, that sums it up okay."

He replied, "This idea is so 'George Carlisle.' I dare say that if George Carlisle himself were sitting here right now, he would be jealous that you thought of it instead of him."

I just smiled. (There went another George Carlisle reference being thrown at me.)

Jonathan contemplated for a few more moments, and then said, "The logistics of this might be more daunting than the basic concept. But I love the basic concept."

I replied, "I know. But we can't let the fear of logistics stop us from doing amazing things."

I continued, "When I returned home to the farm, Eric had a talk with me, similar to what Frank would have done. Eric reminded me of who I am, and who everyone is expecting me to be. I don't want to just sheepishly try to walk in Mrs. Carlisle's and Frank's shoes. I want to DO what they groomed me to do. I want to BE what they groomed me to be. They would expect nothing less than for me to become my own person and push this organization beyond its former limits."

I stopped talking and just looked at Jonathan. He was quiet, still, and thinking.

Then he responded, "I think I have goosebumps."

We laughed, including Rudy.

Jonathan then continued, "I am willing to make anything happen that can possibly be done that is in alignment with your vision."

I replied, "Thank you. I know I can't do any of this without you. But I have some ideas."

I continued, "I know we can't do all of this on our own, nor do I want to. A portion of my vision is to organize events that bring the community together. I am not looking to just offer things on a silver platter for consumption. I want to engineer our events so that it is a catalyst for bringing the community together by having everyone work together for common goals."

I went on, "I want our function to not just be FUNDING the event and the giveaways, but also to facilitate the organizing of volunteers from the community to join us; and also to work with our local businesses to help them when we can, and for them to help us when THEY can."

Jonathan was taking it all in. He responded, "I am listening. I am following you. And I think others will listen to you and follow you also."

I resumed my comments, "Regarding the toy giveaway, I would like you to ask our local trucking company if they would be willing to donate the brief use of some of their trailers for our event. In return, we will of course pay them to do the actual transportation and delivery of the toys to the park."

Jonathan responded, "Yes, good idea. I know the owner of the trucking company because we helped them with one of THEIR events years ago. I know he will help us with this."

I replied, "Good. Next, I realize we don't have the supplier contacts to find a huge variety of toys that we can get here in a timely fashion. HOWEVER, there is that ONE toy store in the neighboring town who surely has all of those supplier connections."

Jonathan responded, "Yes, I know that toy store. It's pretty much the last independently owned toy store in the entire area."

I replied, "Yes. And I want to support them. This is what you need to do. Explain to them what we are doing. Suggest to them that we would like to use their supplier connections, and order all of our toys through them. We will pay them a percentage of our order for their participation, PLUS we will mention them as a co-sponsor of the event, along with the trucking company as well."

Jonathan responded, "Oh my gosh, yes."

I replied, "This will allow us to get all of the toys 'at cost,' but still pay a royalty, if you will, to the toy store for helping us; and in turn give them a nice boost to their 'economy' so that we can keep them around. They are of value to our community, and we should support them."

Jonathan responded, "I think I will just say it to them exactly as you just said it to me."

I replied, "That's fine. My point to all of this will be to show the community that we can all work together to accomplish amazing things."

I paused, and then continued, "Mrs. Carlisle showed me what incredible things are possible. Frank taught me to not keep things, but to give things. My role in moving The Carlisle Trust forward will be to do both of the things that my former mentors taught me, but to also show this community that we are stronger when we all work together. The Carlisle Trust will no longer only be viewed as the organization that does amazing things by giving. We shall also become known for creating fantastic outcomes and opportunities by bringing people, businesses, resources, and volunteers together to do amazing things for all of us, and each other."

I finally stopped speaking. I had a horrible habit of going on for too long. Jonathan was speechless and looked right at Rudy. Rudy got a huge grin on his face and looked down at the table.

Jonathan said to Rudy, "Does he talk like this all of the time, like at the dinner table and stuff?"

Rudy just laughed.

I responded, "No. I'm usually never this smart. It's only when I am inspired by others greater than me who are sitting around me."

After a pause, I added, "In all seriousness, I know this is not going to be easy, and it's not perfect. But I want to try."

Jonathan replied, "No, I agree with you, and I think we need to do this."

I responded, "The tricky part is the distribution, and I will need you to be the genius on this one, Jonathan."

I continued, "My general vision is for us to fill the trucks with a large variety of items that are most popular with kids of different age ranges. Then, we need a system of parents seeing what we have available, and then requesting certain items, and then maybe they are given a slip of paper with a number on it or something. Then when we retrieve the item, they can claim it with the receipt we gave them, or something like that?"

I went on, "I really don't know. You need to be in charge of that part. But I envision volunteers helping us with this, and maybe even dressing up as elves, like they are Santa's helpers getting the toys? And then they can either give the items to the parent, or present it to the child if they are there?"

Jonathan replied, "Yes, that all sounds good, but let me think on it. We have some logistics experts smarter than myself that might come up with something."

Jonathan had another thought, and said, "But what we don't have, and I have no clue about, is how we determine what items and toys to fill the trucks with."

I responded, "Well then, it's a good thing I brought a little elf with me."

Jonathan and I both looked at Rudy.

Jonathan said, "Rudy, do you think that if I gave you a list of different age groups, that you could write down a list of items that are most popular and desired by kids of those age groups?"

Rudy thought for a moment, and replied, "Yes of course, Sir. But you need to tell me how many toys you want me to write down for each group that you assign me."

Jonathan smiled and chuckled. He responded, "Well perhaps we try to think of 10 – 20 items for each age group, but do it for each boys AND girls."

Rudy paused, and replied, "Yes, Sir, I can do that. But for the girls, I have a friend I met at school. Her name is Melissa. She's really nice. I can ask her about the girl's stuff."

Jonathan responded, "PERFECT! But let's keep this a secret Rudy. Let's pretend we are Santa's helpers and we have to keep all of this a secret so that everyone will be surprised. Okay?"

Rudy replied, "I won't tell anyone. Not even Trevor. And I will just tell Melissa I am trying to figure out what presents to give some people."

Jonathan responded, "That's perfect. I will give you the list of age groups before you go, and then you can work on your list and tell me when you are done."

Rudy replied, "Yes, Sir. I will look over your papers just like he does (Rudy pointed at me), and then I will submit my final answers to you just like he does."

Jonathan and I laughed.

Jonathan responded, "That will work, young man. But time is short for us to pull this off, so I will need your list in a couple of days."

Rudy replied, "Yes, Sir."

Jonathan looked at me and said, "Wow, we will have our hands full."

I replied, "Yes we will. And I am not done."

Jonathan responded, "Oh gosh, there is more?"

I replied, "In concert with the toy giveaway, I want to have a large community Christmas festival. I will call it, "Christmas In The Park."

Jonathan looked at me, very intrigued.

I continued, "I want to put up a HUGE Christmas tree at the entrance to the park. Our town has never had an official community Christmas tree. I want to change that. Then, I want to organize a festival that has activities and games for the kids, and beverages and treats for everyone. We can also have the local folks selling their handmade crafts, treats, and things like that. We can have Christmas music, have the kids doing Christmas carols, icing their own Christmas cookies, and create a really festive atmosphere."

Jonathan responded, "WOW!"

I replied, "Yes. And I want to decorate this house, the Carlisle house, like it has never been decorated before. I want it covered in exterior lights, from head to toe. I want The Carlisle Trust, and the park, to become the unofficial 'Christmas Town' of our community."

Jonathan quipped, "WOW!"

I continued, "I want Christmas to be our big annual event where we bring everyone together, and we show the community what Christmas is all about; and in turn, the community shows the world what Christmas is supposed to be all about."

There were a few moments of silence, then Jonathan responded, "I am not sure I have ever been inspired like this before."

He contemplated a bit, and then continued, "Okay, but now it's my turn to contribute a suggestion."

I replied, "Okay. What are you thinking?"

He responded, "I want to do something at this event that allows the community to see YOU. I want you to be seen as the central figure in all of this."

I cringed, and replied, "Oh please no. I am not seeking attention from this. I don't even want any attention."

He responded, "I know. But The Carlisle Trust NEEDS you to be up front in this, and the community needs to build a relationship and bond with you."

I was silent for a bit, and then replied, "What did you have in mind?"

Jonathan pondered. I chuckled within myself, because he literally looked like the Grinch, when the Grinch was thinking about what to do to Whoville.

Finally, I saw a lightbulb go off in Jonathan's head, and he said,

"We will set up a stage with a microphone. Then I want you to do a reading of *The Night Before Christmas* to the entire crowd."

I was stunned at first. I was not sure whether to applaud his creativity, or to throw up in my mouth.

I looked over at Rudy, and Rudy said, "That is the best idea ever!"

I replied to Rudy, "*THAT* is the best idea of everything you have heard today???"

Jonathan started laughing.

Rudy responded, "Yeah, all of the kids will love to see you standing up in front of everyone reading that story."

I looked over at Jonathan, who was looking quite smug and proud of himself.

I said, "I will think about it."

Jonathan looked over at Rudy and said, "You can work on him at home, Rudy."

Rudy nodded in agreement.

I just shook my head. To steal a quote from Frank, "I was in the thick of it now."

Then Jonathan got serious and asked me, "When are you thinking of doing this event?"

I replied, "AH, Good question. What a pesky question of such specific detail."

We both chuckled.

I thought for a moment. I said, "We should do them separately. We should do the toy giveaway as soon as we are able to do it so that parents know what their child has already received from us to go under their tree. But I want to do the Christmas festival on Christmas Eve Day, because this year Christmas Eve Day is on a Saturday. So, let's do it on that Saturday. If we do the same thing next year, we will do it on the Saturday before Christmas Eve Day, or maybe we will just do it on Christmas Eve Day again. Who knows. Let's see how this one goes first."

Jonathan responded, "Sounds reasonable. We will be busy. I need to get our staff working on this right away."

He looked over at Rudy, and said, "Don't forget the toys list, Rudy."

Rudy replied, "I got it. I will have it submitted to you in two days, Sir."

We both laughed. Rudy was just too cute. It was literally impossible to not smile or laugh whenever he spoke in his adult tone.

We adjourned our meeting, and Rudy and I drove back to the farm. After dinner, I spotted Rudy sitting in the parlor study working on his list.

I poked my head in, and said, "Don't forget your regular school homework, also."

He replied, "I know."

Two days later, Rudy said that he had his list done for Jonathan. Jonathan agreed to meet Rudy in the parking lot of his school to get the list from him as he was leaving school and getting into the carpool vehicle to take him home.

A day after that, I started having many phone meetings with Jonathan to coordinate everything. In addition to using the living room as my own private and quiet 'lounging' space, I had also fully taken over the parlor study. I was feeling guilty about monopolizing so much space in Eric and Heather's home. I knew eventually I would have to figure something out. But for the time being, Eric and Heather didn't give any hint of minding the arrangement. I was careful to stay clear of the kitchen and dining room whenever I felt they were having private time between themselves, or with Trevor.

It wasn't long before Jonathan informed me that he had worked everything out regarding the toy giveaway, from acquiring the toys, to delivery, and then having parents choose from what we had available, and then the parents promptly receiving the goods. This was a perfect example of precisely why Jonathan was the Director of Operations for The Carlisle Trust.

Jonathan wanted some guidance from me on how to announce the event. I told him to let the trailer trucks start lining up along the street at the park, and to say nothing, and just let the people in town talk about it for a bit. I told him to only inform the police department of what we were doing.

Sure enough, rumors started raging around town about what the line of trailers could be about. It was amusing to hear all of the various collection of rumors. One of the rumors was that the trailers were full of building supplies, and that I was going to be building a huge mansion for myself in the middle of the park. CRAZY!

However, time was short, and I instructed Jonathan to give a press release to the local newspaper, detailing the toy giveaway event. It made the front page. The headline read, "Christmas comes early thanks to The Carlisle Trust."

There was a huge outpouring of support. Although I had asked Jonathan to be the 'front-man' for the toy giveaway event, he ended up giving me full credit for the event, and mentioning my name over and over again in the press release. It made me shake my head, as I should have known he would do that.

It was very positive press for me and The Carlisle Trust, but there was something about so much attention, and receiving credit for things that still made me uncomfortable. Remember, I was the kid who tried his best to remain invisible all through high school.

I was being hailed as a 'hero' for providing a good Christmas to many of our local families; but I was wanting to shift this attention to focus upon the community as a whole. The entire point of this was not to become a hero, but to bring our community together so that our community would become its own hero to its own citizens. It was for this precise reason that I decided to agree to the public appearance at the "Christmas in the Park" festival. Perhaps it would be my chance to address the community as to my intentions behind my actions.

I decided to stay silent and invisible until then. I had Jonathan handle the toy giveaway, with him as the public face of The Carlisle Trust for that event. He deserved it anyway, because he, along with his AMAZING staff, had somehow managed to pull together the event.

The toy giveaway was a tremendous success. There was a huge line of people on both days that we did the event. The line moved quickly, and it seemed like everyone was satisfied with what they received. There was a mix of parents there alone to secretly get gifts for their children, but also a few parents who showed up with their kids.

We had given away more toys in two days than anyone could recall ever happening, under any circumstances, anywhere in our area. Best of all, we never ran out. We actually had plenty of toys left over. Jonathan asked me what I wanted done with them. I decided that we would keep them, and give them away throughout the year to families that suffered losses due to fire, domestic abuse issues, economic hardships, or any other good causes. I instructed him to also make them available to other surrounding communities and charitable groups for similar purposes.

After the trailers were removed from the park, we went to work installing the Christmas tree and putting up as many decorations and lights as our electrical infrastructure could handle. The park became a real center of the town, with many people making a special trip to the park just to see the tree. I pledged that the following year, we would be doing all of this much earlier so that the town could enjoy it for much longer.

Jonathan was deep into the planning and setting up of the next event, which would be the festival to be held on Christmas Eve Day.

I let him do what he did best, while I stayed at home and pondered what I wanted to say, at what would be my first official public appearance and address since taking over The Carlisle Trust.

Meanwhile, life went on as usual at the farm. Rudy and Trevor were out back in the woods having their own discussions and contemplations. Trevor was showing Rudy, for the first time, his secret fort that he had built up in the woods.

Rudy said, "Wow Trevor, this is a cool fort. When did you build this?"

Trevor replied, "After everyone left at the end of summer when farm camp ended. I was bored and didn't have anyone my own age to hang out with, so I started coming up here in the woods to think. I decided I wanted to build a fort so that I could have a cool place to be alone that nobody knew about."

After a moment, Trevor added, "But what this fort needs now is a Christmas decoration. We should make a Christmas wreath for it."

Rudy responded, "I don't know how to do that."

Trevor replied, "I do. Eric taught me. We made one together for the farmhouse. All you do is gather some fir tips, especially balsam if you can find them, and then you twist them all together into a circle."

Rudy responded, "Okay, let's try."

The boys started looking around for the best materials to use. Rudy watched Trevor at first, and then got the idea of what type of fir tips to get, and what to harvest for supplies. The boys gathered what they needed, and went back to the fort to assemble them into a wreath.

Rudy watched Trevor start the assembly process, but then he jumped in and started to help once he saw how it was done. Before too long, the boys had completed the wreath. Trevor found the perfect place to hang it, and did so in a very ceremonious way.

After a few moments of admiring their fine holiday work of art,

Rudy asked, "What do you think about when you're here alone?"

Trevor replied, "Everything that's happened to me. Like what happened to my entire family, my brother, my mom, and my dad."

He continued, "My entire family is dead. I am the only one left, and I'm an orphan."

Rudy thought for a moment, and responded, "I guess I'm an orphan also."

Trevor replied, "Yeah, I guess that's right. So, we're both orphans together."

Rudy responded, "I never even had a dad. My dad left me and my mom when I was really little, and I only saw him briefly on and off a few times. I never had anyone to call 'dad' in my entire life."

After a pause, he added, "I guess no dad has ever wanted me."

Trevor replied, "Yeah but you have a really cool foster parent now. He's practically famous."

Rudy responded, "Yeah but I still don't have anyone to call dad."

Trevor replied, "Yeah, I understand. I love Eric and Heather, but I don't call them 'mom and dad' because they are my foster parents."

He continued, "I love being with them, and I love living here, but sometimes I still get sad that I'm an orphan. No matter what, I will always be an orphan."

After a pause, Rudy responded, "Trevor, do you believe in magic?"

Trevor immediately replied, "No! Why would I? Nothing magical has ever happened to me. The only thing that has happened to me my entire life is all of my family dying, one at a time. What is magical about that?"

Rudy responded, "Magic is not about things that already happened to you. Magic is about what CAN happen to you in the future. Magic is about BELIEVING that something CAN happen, and then sometimes it happens, and *that* is magical. But you have to believe first. If you don't believe, then magic can't happen."

After thinking about that for a moment, Trevor replied, "Hmmm, well I don't think anything magical can happen to me."

Rudy responded, "Will you at least try it, Trevor?"

Trevor replied, "What do you mean? How do I do it?"

Rudy thought for a moment, and responded, "Let's use this Christmas wreath that we both just made together. I think it's magical."

He continued, "Let's both make a wish to this wreath. But you have to try and BELIEVE IT, Trevor."

Trevor hesitantly replied, "Okay, but what should we wish?"

Before Rudy could answer, Trevor said, "Let's wish that someday we won't be orphans."

Rudy responded, "That's a tough one, Trevor. We can't change what has already happened."

Trevor replied in a somewhat snarky tone, "Hey, I thought you said this was magic? If it's magic, then anything can happen, so you claim."

Rudy, with his hopes and enthusiasm slightly deflated, responded, "Okay. We can try, I guess."

After a moment of focus, Rudy said, "Stare at the wreath and focus on your wish. Think of nothing else except for your wish. Okay?"

Trevor replied, "Okay. Tell me when to start."

Rudy quipped, "NOW!"

Both of the boys stared intently at the wreath with all of their might.

After a minute that seemed like five minutes had gone by, Rudy said, "Okay, stop."

Trevor replied, "I did as you said."

Rudy responded, "Well, I guess we wait to see what happens."

Trevor replied, "I like that we tried. I like your ideas, Rudy."

Rudy responded, "Thanks."

Trevor then said, "But in case it doesn't work and we are always orphans, can we make a promise to each other?"

Rudy replied, "Sure. Like what?"

Trevor responded, "Let's always promise that we will be here for each other, like brothers."

He continued, "I'm pretty sure we will always see each other forever."

Rudy replied, "How do you know that?"

Trevor responded, "Because I heard Eric talking to Heather one time about your foster parent. Eric said that he would follow him into a burning building, even if it meant that he wouldn't make it out alive."

He continued, "I think that means Eric and your foster father will always be friends forever, and THAT means you and I can be friends forever."

Rudy replied, "Good point. I guess you're right. I heard my foster father say that if it was not for Eric, there would be no way he could have continued on after all of his losses."

Trevor responded, "Let's you and me be friends just like they are!"

Rudy replied, "Yes, I like that!"

Trevor responded, "Good, I'm glad it's settled. But can we go back to the house now cause I'm hungry."

Rudy laughed, and replied, "Okay, me too."

The boys took one last look at their Christmas wreath, and then started heading back to the house.

Once back at the house, the boys didn't speak again of their pact they had made at the fort in the woods. Rudy only told me what had happened long after that Christmas had passed.

Before I knew it, Christmas Eve Day had arrived. It was my big, dreaded, exciting day to make my appearance at the park for the

"Christmas in the Park" festival. I was very nervous. In principle, I loved the idea of getting directly involved with the public, and I knew I needed to make more public appearances. But now that the day had finally arrived, I found myself regretting that I had agreed to do it. It wasn't because I didn't want to be involved, but rather because I was always nervous about things like this. For example, I was a total nervous wreck over Mrs. Carlisle's funeral, and I didn't even need to say anything for that. Now, imagine how nervous I was knowing that I had to make a speech AND read a book to a crowd. YIKES!

Plus, I had no idea what to wear. I think in my mind I was just going to show up in jeans, a t-shirt, and sneakers. But once reality hit, I knew I couldn't do that. But was I supposed to wear a suit? Really?? All of this was making me even more nervous than I should have been.

Once Eric was back in the house from doing chores, I said, "Eric! Help!"

He laughed at me, as if he knew, and was expecting me to be all tied up in knots over this event.

I said to him, "I know what I am saying, but I don't know what I'm wearing, or how I should act. All of this is just so awkward for me."

He stared at me, and thought for a moment.

Then he said, "You have to ingratiate yourself to the crowd, but just be you. You have to own it. It will be the only way through this for you."

I replied annoyingly, "What does that even mean? Do you have an English version of that available?"

Eric responded, "Wait here. Let me get something."

Eric went upstairs, and then quickly came back down with what looked like a sweater of some sort.

He handed it to me, and said, "Own it."

I unfurled the sweater-garment-thing, and took a full look at what he had given me. It was a really ugly Christmas sweater.

I said, "Are you kidding me?"

He chuckled, and responded, "Nope. You need to wear this sweater, and you need to wear it with pride."

I just stared at him. I knew he was being serious. It took me a good minute to think it over. Then I finally realized what I thought he was thinking, or trying to do, with me wearing that sweater.

I said, "I see what you're doing here. It might work. This sweater is so horrible that it takes all of the pressure off of me in a way."

He responded, "Yep. Anyone wearing that sweater can't take himself too seriously, and therefore, the audience won't hold you to a higher more serious standard like they would a politician, for example."

I replied, "Yeah, this is smart. See, this is why I need you."

He grinned. But I had more questions.

I asked, "So do I wear jeans with this, or what?"

He responded, "NO! You wear business slacks. The sweater says that you are not taking yourself too seriously and are having fun with the season and festival; but the business slacks say that you still have class and authority."

I replied, "Okay."

After a moment, I said, "So, can I wear my sneakers with this?"

Heather, who had since peeked in on the conversation, yelled, "NO! OH MY GOSH, you can't wear sneakers! You need nice shoes."

I replied, "So I should wear the shoes from the funeral? They're all I have."

Heather responded, "Yes, those will work."

Eric then said, "Dude, you need to go do some clothes shopping. Are you waiting for people to take up a collection for you first or what?"

I replied, "No, I'm happy with the clothes I have, so why would I need more?"

Eric responded, "You are not some college kid walking around the beach anymore."

I thought about what he said. The odd thing was that in my own mind, I WAS INDEED still a college kid walking around a beach. I guess Eric was right and I needed to reevaluate my 'look.'

I replied, "Okay, thanks guys. Got it. I think I can handle putting them on myself, but then again, maybe not."

We all laughed, and I added, "Thanks for nursing me along."

While we were all together, we discussed our plans for the day. We would take separate vehicles, because after the event, Rudy and I were going to my parents, and Eric, Heather, and Trevor were going to Eric's mom's house. I asked Eric and Heather to keep an eye on Rudy during the time that I would be occupied at the event.

Rudy and I ended up leaving for the festival well in advance, because I wanted to get to the Carlisle house early so that I could speak with Jonathan and make sure I was ready for all of this.

Once Eric and family arrived, they sent Trevor over to the Carlisle house to get Rudy. Rudy and Trevor had fun together at the festival, while Eric and Heather got to look around at the various crafts, and just take it easy together almost like it was a date.

I was very nervous, and Jonathan must have known this. He was trying to divert my attention and make small-talk to keep me calm while we waited for when I needed to walk over to the main stage. It was one of those times, again, when I felt I needed to use the restroom over and over again to make sure I was all good.

Eventually, one of Jonathan's people whispered into his ear, and Jonathan told me it was time to head over. We left the Carlisle house and were escorted into the park by several staff members.

As we were walking toward the stage area, Jonathan said, "That is the worst sweater I have ever seen."

I replied, "I know! Eric made me wear it!"

Jonathan responded, "It's brilliant! Eric is brilliant, as always."

At first, I wasn't sure if he was joking or serious. But I could see that he was being serious.

He then said, "If you get nervous, just look down at your sweater. You can't take any of this too seriously wearing a sweater like that."

I replied, "That's what Eric said."

Jonathan responded, "I know. That's why Eric is so brilliant."

I tried to do as he suggested, and it kind of worked. It was hard to be too tense and uptight wearing such a hideous sweater.

Jonathan and his staff led me to the back of the stage. Jonathan went up to the microphone and did a very short welcoming speech to the crowd, and then he introduced me.

I walked up onto the stage wearing my silly Christmas sweater. People clapped and were staring at me, likely wondering what in the world I would say while wearing such an outrageously offensive sweater.

It's safe to say that most everyone in town had heard about me, but almost nobody in town actually KNEW me. Thus, there was a certain level of curiosity about me.

I began my public address as follows:

Merry Christmas everyone. Welcome to what is our first, and we hope annual, 'Christmas in the Park' festival. I stand before you under very bitter-sweet circumstances. This past year we lost two of the most valued members of our community; and I lost my two mentors who taught me what compassion, generosity, discipline, and dignity were truly about.

I stand here humbled, unable to replace who and what we all lost as a community. But I also stand here as a member of this community, wanting to do everything within my power to make it a better place for all of us.

Like everyone, I will make mistakes, and I may falter from time to time. But I want to pledge to all of you today that I will always do what I feel is right for each and every one of us, and most especially for our children.

I cannot stand here like Mr. and Mrs. Carlisle and claim to be a parent or grandparent to all of you as they did, and as they were. I am obviously a bit too young for that, and I have not yet earned your respect, which the Carlisle's were fully deserving of. But what I CAN do, is stand here and say that I consider all of you my family.

As the new Principal Trustee of The Carlisle Trust, my mission is going to be to use all of the resources available to me to help my 'family,' which is all of you. However, I won't do it alone. I will need your help. In fact, I humbly beg for your help. I ask you for your help in allowing all of us to come together as a community, as one family, and work together to make things better for all of us.

Your personal efforts will become my inspiration to work harder, and to be better in serving this community. I am certain that if we all work together and treat each other as family, that we will ensure the creation of the greatest community that perhaps our great nation has ever seen. We can be the model of how things should be, and can be. But we can only accomplish this if all of us work together. Is there anyone here today who agrees with me at all, with any of this??"

I wasn't sure what was going to happen next. In my nightmares, I pictured either complete silence, or even some booing. Neither of that happened. Instead, the ENTIRE crowd ROARED, "YES!" The crowd then started chanting, "YES! YES! YES!"

I eventually had to interrupt them, as I wondered if they would ever stop chanting, "YES!"

I resumed speaking, and said, "You have all touched my heart, and I thank you for your love and support. I also thank you for your love and support toward your neighbors and your community. But I have bored everyone here enough, and I think it's time for a reading of *The Night Before Christmas*. Shall we?"

Everyone erupted in cheers. Jonathan, who had been standing behind me the entire time, handed me the book.

I read the book as best as I could. I didn't make any major fumbles, thank goodness. When I was finished, there were no 'boos,' thankfully. There were only cheers.

Just as I was about to step off the stage, there were some members of the crowd who started yelling things very loudly. I wondered if I was being heckled. But then I started hearing some of the things they were yelling. They were things like, "Thank you for the toys!" "You saved our Christmas!" "You gave us a good Christmas for our kids!"

I stayed at the microphone. I was not looking for praise or credit. I wanted to make a point.

During a gap in the crowd yelling things, I said, "Thank you. But this was a community effort. We had businesses who contributed, and we had volunteers who gave of their time, and of themselves. We ALL did this. We need to give thanks and gratitude to each other. We are all family here, and we all did this together. God bless you all and have a very Merry Christmas."

I walked off the stage to lots of cheering. I had chills running up and down my spine. I was somewhat uncomfortable, and somewhat embarrassed, but I was also very humbled, grateful, inspired, and I felt warmth and love. I felt that however weird the experience had just been, that maybe I had done the right things, said the right things, and I was grateful it had been well received.

Jonathan was beaming from ear to ear, so I took that to mean I had done okay. Once Rudy ran behind the stage to join me, Jonathan and a number of others ushered us away from the stage and back to the Carlisle house. As we were walking back to the house, we could hear a new chant from the crowd. It was, "YES! THANK

YOU!" They chanted it over and over until we were inside the Carlisle house.

I had never experienced anything like that in my life. The public memorial for Mrs. Carlisle was the closest comparable thing; but this Christmas event seemed much more personal, and came with a deeper connection between me and the community. There were literally no words to fully express the deep feelings and gratitude I felt in those moments.

Years later, Jonathan would say that he believed that speech was when the magic really began. But who knows, and I won't speak of any spoilers of things to come.

Once inside the Carlisle house, we all had some beverages and treats to unwind from the chaos. I was just waiting for things to calm down a bit so that Rudy and I could discreetly get down the street to my parent's house.

I assumed that my parents had gone to the event, although I had not seen them. I wanted to give them ample time to return home before Rudy and I would be knocking on their door to enjoy our annual Christmas Eve dinner at their house.

Once I felt that Rudy and I could drive the short distance down the street without everyone in the world seeing where my parents lived, I started saying my goodbyes to Jonathan and The Carlisle Trust staff that were present in the house. I had already given out Christmas bonuses to everyone who worked for The Carlisle Trust, but I wanted to thank them personally for their fantastic work. I went around the house, upstairs and downstairs, and wished everyone a Merry Christmas, and thanked them from the bottom of my heart for all of their work.

Lastly, Rudy and I wished Jonathan a Merry Christmas, and I congratulated him on an amazingly successful Christmas season. He had pulled off two major events flawlessly. I was very pleased and relieved that everything had worked out so well, but I was mostly incredibly grateful that I was fortunate enough to work with such an amazing and talented group of people. I was just one tiny piece of the whole thing. Jonathan made it his mission to see that I got most of the credit, but almost all of the credit belonged to Jonathan and The Carlisle Trust staff, along with our partners.

By the way, in future years more and more people showed up to the event wearing ugly Christmas sweaters. It became part of the festival. They have Eric to thank (or curse) for that.

Rudy and I arrived at my parent's house and knocked on the door. My mom answered, and her eyes went immediately to Rudy, and she said, "WELCOME! I'M SO HAPPY TO SEE YOU AGAIN!"

Rudy smiled and said, "Thank you, Ma'am."

Rudy walked inside; and fortunately, I was able to scoot inside behind him before my mother could shut the door in my face. But once inside, my mother seemed to notice I was there also, and she suggested I get a drink for myself, and something for Rudy as well.

I could smell that dinner seemed to be very close to being ready. My mom had cooked everything before the festival. She knew I was on a tight schedule. Normally, I would be at my parent's house all day for Christmas Eve, but because of the festival, we only had enough time for dinner, and then Rudy and I needed to get back to the farm before it got too late.

Eric, Heather, and Trevor had left from the festival to go to Eric's mom's place, with the same idea in mind of having dinner, and then going back to the farm at a reasonable hour. I'm sure they must have left right after my speech was over.

My mom instructed me to bring some of the food items out to the dining room table, and I did so. She announced dinner was ready, and my stepfather ambled on in from the living room.

He smiled at Rudy, and said, "Hey there Sport!"

Rudy replied, "Hi, Sir."

We all sat down at the table. My stepfather said a short prayer. It was a real formal prayer, not like the one we said at the farm.

We all started digging in, but I prepared a plate for Rudy first so that he didn't have to reach, hoping this would prevent any mishaps.

As always, my mom had cooked a roast beast, which looked incredible, and cooked exactly to my liking. We enjoyed our food for, what, maybe three minutes?

Then my stepfather broke the silence, and said in his standard authoritative tone, "That was quite a speech you gave."

I replied, "Thanks?"

Then He said, "It sounded like someone who might be getting into politics. It almost sounded like you were poliTICKing."

I replied, "Nope. I wasn't poliTICKing."

He grunted and responded, "Well maybe you should."

I replied, "Nope. I don't like politics."

He responded, "Well. Let's just pretend for a moment that you DID go into politics. Which political party would you run as?"

I replied, "Neither. I don't like politics."

He responded, "Well I would need to know which party you would be running as in order for me to decide whether or not to vote for you."

I responded, "I think we already know how you would vote in that situation."

My mom, feeling that the temperature in the room had risen enough, jumped in, and said loudly, "SO RUDY, HOW HAS SCHOOL BEEN FOR YOU?"

Rudy replied, "Good. I like my school, and I like my friends there. Plus, Trevor goes there with me."

My mom responded, "Who is Trevor?"

I looked at her and said, "Remember mom, Trevor is the kid that Eric and Heather took in. He is the Winters child, the younger one. He lives at the farm with us."

I had already told my mother this a long time ago. But she looked at me and said, "Well, you never tell me anything, so I don't know what is going on. I have no idea."

Not wanting to argue with her, I just said, "Yeah, Trevor lives at the farm with us."

My stepfather jumped back in and said, "How long are all of you going to live in that communal setting, all together at that farm?"

I sighed, and replied, "I don't know. A lot has happened to me in the last nine months. I can barely keep up with it myself. For right now, it's working out really well, and we live together as a family quite efficiently."

My stepfather grunted.

My mom said, "Rudy, I have some special Christmas cookies for us to eat after dinner."

Rudy replied, "Oh excellent, thank you."

My stepfather looked at Rudy and said, "You really are a delightful young man, aren't you?"

Rudy, not knowing how to react to that, just gave out an awkward giggle and a smile.

After dinner, we went into the living room and opened up some presents. It was very pleasant. For my gift to them, I offered to do some upgrades to their kitchen, and asked them to think about what they might want. They gave Rudy some really cute stuff, considering that they didn't know much about him.

After the gifts, I felt pretty good about the visit, and decided we should make our exit while things were still on a positive note. I hesitated a moment before getting up from the couch though, because I was taking in their beautiful Christmas tree, and my mom's traditional Christmas music that I had grown up with. There was something very grounding about it that reminded me of who I was. If only I could have just sat there for a while to enjoy it, without the risk of getting into an unpleasant tangle with them, it would have been nice.

But Rudy seemed happy, and they both had been very kind and gentle toward Rudy. However 'unpleasant?' my visits could sometimes be, there was still something I liked about being back 'home' for Christmas Eve. However, it was definitely time to get going, so that we could be back home at the farm in time to unwind, and for the kids to get to bed. I'm sure Eric and the others had already headed back as well. Eric hated to be gone from the farm too long because of all the animals.

Rudy and I got ready to leave. I waved to my stepfather, who waved back. Then he looked at Rudy and said, "Nice to see you again, young man. I hope to see you again soon, okay?"

Rudy replied, "Yes, okay."

When we were at the door, my mom asked, "So when might we see you again?"

In my mind, I had no idea. But in my words, I said, "We can stop by again when you want, because we're often down the street for meetings at The Carlisle house."

My mom responded, "WE? You make that child go to those big adult business meetings with you?"

I replied, "Yes mom, Rudy goes to the meetings because he wants to."

She gave me one of her disapproving looks, and responded, "That just seems weird to me. He's just a child."

I didn't want to argue. I just wanted to LEAVE. So, I said, "It's okay mom. Don't worry about it. We'll see you soon. Contact me any time."

Then I just moved my legs and herded Rudy out the door. I gave a wave as I HURRIED to the car. We made a swift exit from the driveway, and I gave out a huge sigh of relief. Rudy was watching all of this.

He said, "Wow, your relationship with your parents is 'interesting.'

I started laughing. I replied, "Yes, good way to put it, Rudy."

We made it back to the farm; and as I suspected, Eric, Heather, and Trevor had already returned. We went inside, and Eric was amusingly awaiting my report. He knew of all the dynamics between me and my parents, and he found it entertaining.

He was already in the living room next to the fireplace. He knew where I would be going! I got some hot tea and joined him, while Heather was trying to get the boys settled so that they would get to bed soon.

Eric, with a big grin on his face, said, "So how was *THAT?*"

I replied, "The good news is that they were both very kind to Rudy. The other news is that nothing has changed with them, and I was lucky to escape with my sanity."

I continued, "My stepfather was trying to say that my speech at the festival was political, and that I surely must be running for office; and he demanded to know which political party I would be running as."

Eric started laughing.

He paused, and then he responded, "That speech. Wow. I didn't see it as political. BUT that speech has now made it so that there is no going back for you. You have turned yourself into a 'thing' with your performance today. I'm surprised there isn't a crowd of people out on the front lawn right now as we speak."

I laughed and replied, "Thank you. It felt good. It felt right. For the first time, I felt like I was who I was, if that makes any sense."

Eric responded, "It does. I get it. And believe me, YOU ARE who you are now. So, you better stay on your game from now on."

I replied, "Oh thanks for the extra pressure. Appreciate it."

He chuckled and responded, "I'm just saying it was a huge performance, and it has elevated you to another level now."

He paused, and then said, "Mrs. Carlisle and Frank would be very impressed."

I replied, "I hope so."

After that, we changed the subject and made small-talk about other things, and he filled me in with the latest on his mom. Eric and I enjoyed some nice time together. I had a fleeting thought that what I was enjoying with Eric in that moment, on Christmas Eve night, was EXACTLY the same as what I had enjoyed with Frank. It was comforting and heartwarming for me.

Heather had managed to get the boys to bed, and she had gone up to bed also without interrupting the moment Eric and I were enjoying. It wasn't long though before Eric bailed on me, because he was really tired and was used to going to bed early.

He made his exit, and I wished him a Merry Christmas, which he reciprocated. I sat alone next to the fireplace staring at the tree. I was once again reminded of how fortunate I was that things had turned out the way they did. It was not many months ago that I was at a personal low and in complete despair. But that had all changed in such an enormous and wonderful way.

I said, "Merry Christmas Frank," out loud, before shutting all of the lights off and heading upstairs to bed.

The next morning when I came downstairs and went into the living room, our glorious Christmas tree was all lit up and looking magical. It appeared that Santa had visited, because there were two stockings hanging by the fireplace that were stuffed with gifts. I had a funny feeling that Santa must have had help from Heather in some way.

The stockings were fantastic! They looked to be possibly handmade. They were made of very soft and furry flannel material for the "stocking part," and then there was an even fluffier white wrapping of material at the top of the stocking around the top opening. Sewn onto the white part were the names of the boys. One stocking saying "Trevor," and the other saying "Rudy." How amazingly wonderful and kind [of Heather].

The boys seemed anxious to dive into their stockings and see what treasures were inside, but I think they felt they needed permission first. This was our first Christmas all together, and there were no set rules or protocols of how to do things yet.

For me personally, when I was a child, I would be up at 5:00AM tearing into my stocking alone while my parents slept. But Trevor and Rudy didn't know what the routine was for our Christmases and showed restraint in waiting.

The stockings aside, what had REALLY caught the interest of the boys, were the two boxes sitting under the tree. And those were the ONLY two gifts under the tree. Eric, Heather, and I had already coordinated and agreed on what we were doing for this Christmas. The three of us decided to just give each of the boys one gift. This would not always be the policy for our future Christmases, but it would be what we did for *this* Christmas.

There was nothing else under the tree. Just two boxes of the exact same size, both wrapped in the exact same Christmas paper, with the exact same big bow on the top. The only difference between the two gifts was that one had a tag on it that said it was to Trevor from Eric and Heather, while the other gift had a tag that said it was to Rudy from myself.

We saw the boys picking up the boxes to feel them, and they even gave them a gentle shake. The boys were totally mystified as to what could be inside the boxes. They both remarked at how the boxes felt as light as a feather, and that there were no detectable noises or rattles coming from the boxes when shaken.

Trevor even said, "Did you get us AIR for Christmas?"

We all laughed. Eric replied, "Yes, Trevor, I can confirm that there IS air in the box."

We were all laughing as Trevor gave him a look of slight annoyance.

Rudy and Trevor wouldn't stop staring at the boxes. Rudy was equally as intrigued, but he was less vocal about it. Eventually, Trevor came out and asked Heather when they could open up the boxes.

Heather replied, "The four of you boys have chores to do first. The animals come first."

Eric had already made an announcement the prior night that we didn't need to wake up until 6:00AM, because with the four of us doing the chores together, we could get it all done quickly.

He was right. One person doing the chores alone was a real time-consuming task, and could be quite lonely, although as a farmer you become comfortable with it, and even like the peace and solitude. But doing chores with another person was so much better, as I knew from my time with Frank and Eric, and as Eric knew from doing them with me and Trevor. However, doing them with even more people was even more fun, and it meant they got done very quickly.

The four of us guys went outside with our hot beverages and started in. Trevor and Rudy fed the animals while Eric and I did the shoveling out and cleaning out. We all made fun small-talk, and Eric and I enjoyed listening to Trevor teaching Rudy more about how to feed all of the animals. While Rudy was not a complete stranger to the farm, he had not been very involved with the chores. Since we had been staying there, Eric pretty much kept the chores to himself and Trevor.

We all completed everything in no time at all. Once we were all back inside from doing the chores, had cleaned up, and were back downstairs, Trevor asked Heather again when they could open the two gifts under the tree.

Heather responded, "Why don't you see what Santa left in the stockings first?"

It should be noted that the boys were old enough to know what was likely going on with the stockings. But they were still enthusiastic about the 'magic of Santa,' still the same. The boys took down their stockings from the fireplace and started digging in and unwrapping the contents piece by piece.

There were a variety of treasures, such as candy, chocolate, little amusing toys, and trinkets. It was the normal Christmas stocking that you would expect for boys of their age. They both seemed amused by what they got, although you could see them still eyeing the two boxes under the tree out of the corner of their eyes.

While the kids were busy with their stockings, Heather had put out all kinds of breakfast treats for us to enjoy, along with my favorite hot tea. However, I was so anxious about the gifts under the tree, I didn't have much of an appetite. If I am to be honest, I might have been equally excited about the gifts as the kids. I think Eric and Heather felt the same.

Heather glanced at me, and then Eric, as if wondering whether we should just get it over with. We were all so tied up in knots that we were not relaxing and eating all of the great food. Heather got little nods of approval from both me and Eric. She then grabbed her camera because she wanted to get some pictures of the kids as they each opened up their only Christmas gift.

Heather looked over at the kids and said, "Are you guys ready to open your gift?"

The kids immediately exclaimed, "YES!"

Those were the words they had been waiting for one of us adults to say.

The kids ran over to the tree and kneeled down next to the two gifts. They could see that Heather was wanting to get some pictures. Both Trevor and Rudy posed for some pictures, kneeling down next to each other with big smiles, while each of them were holding their respective gifts.

The boys looked at Heather for one last confirmation that it was okay for them to start. Eric and I sat silently, as if invisible, watching every moment of what was unfolding before us.

Heather nodded to the boys, and said, "Go ahead."

Trevor and Rudy both looked at each other, and gave each other a smile of anticipatory excitement. Then, as if they had decided to open their gifts together in exact synchronicity, they started pulling at the wrapping paper and unwrapping the boxes at the same speed as each other.

Once the wrapping paper was off, the boys could see that they were each holding an ornamental box with its own "wrapping" printed on the box. However, all that was left to do was to pull off the top cover of the box.

Each boy looked at each other again, and then started to lift up the top cover at the same time. They did this, and once the top covers were off, the boys looked inside the boxes.

There was perhaps a four second pause of no reaction from the boys as they were processing what they were looking at.

Rudy was the first to react, but only by about one second or less before Trevor. Both boys' eyes turned red, their bodies started to tremble, and then tears started streaming down their cheeks.

They just sat there, frozen in that moment. For Eric, Heather, and myself, it felt like an eternity, as if that moment was truly frozen in time. Those two boys were sitting side-by-side, staring into each of their boxes, trembling, while their breathing started to become irregular, and tears were streaming down their cheeks.

What was inside the boxes?

In Trevor's box, there was simply one piece of paper. In Rudy's box, there was also simply, one piece of paper.

Written on Trevor's piece of paper was the phrase, "We are adopting you." Written on Rudy's piece of paper was the phrase, "I am adopting you."

The boys continued staring down at the words written on the pieces of paper in a complete state of tears. Then what happened next surprised all of us.

I truly expected that perhaps the boys would come running over to each of us for hugs. That did not happen. Instead, the boys, in all of their tears, looked over at each other at the same exact moment, and they embraced each other. They hugged each other, held each other, and cried together.

Heather took in a huge gasp as she put her hand up to her mouth and started crying. It was so surprising, so shocking, so amazing, so touching, that I completely lost it. I couldn't help it. Tears were falling out of my eyes. But Heather and I were not the only ones. The same was true for Eric as well.

I do not know how long this moment, this embrace between the two boys lasted. But it felt like a long time, as I was trying to mop tears from my eyes.

Finally, the boys broke their embrace, and Trevor ran over to Eric and Heather. With a gigantic smile on his face, he hugged both of them. Then all three of them hugged together.

As for Rudy, he walked over to me slowly and gently, completely overwhelmed with emotion. He softly sunk into my waiting arms. I embraced him. Then he started crying uncontrollably. He was absolutely overwhelmed with the emotion that had consumed him. It didn't feel to me that he was only crying out of joy from opening up his Christmas gift. It felt to me that he was releasing many years worth of emotions that had been bottled up inside him for most of his life. It felt so incredibly cathartic and intense for him.

He was crying so intensely that he was convulsing with his breathing. He held me tighter than I had ever felt him hold me before. He would not lighten his grip on me. I continued to hold him tightly as I stroked the back of his head, trying to calm him down.

After Trevor left his embrace with Eric and Heather, he saw Rudy having that deeply emotional moment with me. Trevor walked over to us, and he started rubbing Rudy's back.

Then Trevor said to Rudy, "You were right about magic, Rudy. I believe in magic now. You were right."

This got Rudy to calm down enough to look over at Trevor. The boys made eye contact and smiled at each other. This caused Rudy to calm down a bit more. He broke his death-grip on me and just stood before me next to Trevor, as he was trying to calm himself down.

Trevor put his hand on Rudy's shoulder and said, "We won't be orphans anymore, Rudy."

This caused Rudy to start crying harder again, and it caused Eric and Heather to start with *their* tears again.

Rudy just nodded his head in acknowledgement of Trevor's statement.

As Rudy was struggling to calm down, Trevor was only showing excitement and glee.

He looked over at Eric and Heather and asked, "Does this mean I can call you mom and dad?"

Not having a calm, sane moment to get control of ourselves, myself, Eric, and Heather still had tears, and Eric was the one who was able to pull himself together enough to reply, "Yes, Son."

Trevor ran back over to them, and said, "I love you Mom and Dad."

The three of them embraced again.

At this rate, there was no way any of us were EVER going to stop crying. It seemed as if there was no end in sight. It was like when someone says something so funny that you are laughing really hard, and then someone else says something more funny to add to it, and everyone laughs even more, and it goes on until nobody can breathe. This was the exact same thing, except with crying. I know Eric and I were trying to stop, but it was just one thing after another.

Finally, Rudy calmed down enough to speak. He looked at me

and said, "What about me?"

I replied, "What do you mean?"

He started crying a bit again, but choked out the words, "Can I call you dad?" Then he grabbed me and started crying much harder again.

I let him cry for a moment, and then when I felt he could hear me and understand what I was saying, I replied, "Of course, Son."

Rudy stayed in our embrace for quite a while. Eventually, he broke away again and started to really calm down.

I think at that point, we were all praying that the tears would end, at least for us adults. I honestly had expected an emotional moment, but I thought it was just going to be a quick hug after the kids opened the boxes. It turned into an epic ever-lasting moment instead.

Once we had all calmed down and had dry eyes, Trevor exclaimed, "There is nothing else I could have wanted more than this! THIS IS THE BEST CHRISTMAS IN THE WORLD!"

Rudy nodded in agreement.

This is when I decided it might be the right moment for me to spring my own secret surprise on everyone. I had something up my sleeve that I had not even told Eric and Heather about.

In reply to Trevor's comment about him being totally satisfied with his one and only gift, I said, "So I guess this means you might have zero interest in what I have hidden behind the far shed then?"

Trevor's head quickly swiveled over to me, and he said, "There is something hidden behind the far shed??"

I replied, "I believe so."

The "far shed" was just one of the outbuildings used for storage, and it was called the "far shed," because it was the shed farthest from the house.

Eric and Heather looked over at me with looks of shock and curiosity.

Eric said, "What have you done now?"

I replied, "We will never know because nobody cares to go look."

Trevor yelled, "I'LL GO LOOK!"

Then he added, "COME WITH ME RUDY! LET'S GO!"

The boys threw on some boots and jackets, and started running outside. I motioned for Eric and Heather to follow me outside. I figured we would just stand outside the house and watch them run over to the far shed.

Eric and Heather waited with intense anticipation to see what would happen once the boys arrived behind the shed.

The boys reached the shed, and then ran behind it, out of our view. There was a short gap of silence, but then we heard Trevor yelling and cheering. I started laughing because I realized that Eric and Heather still had no idea of what was going on yet. All they could hear was Trevor screaming in euphoric excitement. Rudy was never a 'screamer,' so I was not surprised that we didn't hear anything from Rudy.

After some moments of celebratory yelling from Trevor, the boys both came running back over to the house where we were standing. Trevor was yelling about something, but we still couldn't understand him. It was totally hilarious for me to watch Eric and Heather being tortured by still having no clear answers as to what was going on. I wouldn't help them either. I just kept laughing.

When the boys were back to us, everyone could clearly see the joy and excitement on both boys' faces. Rudy was indeed very excited.

Trevor went right up to Eric and said, "ERIC! I MEAN DAD! IT'S A BRAND-NEW ATV! A FOUR-WHEELER! IT'S HUGE, A BIG ONE. A FANCY ONE!"

Eric looked over at me with his 'Eric look' that he would give me whenever I had done something for him. I just smiled and laughed.

Then I made an announcement. I said, "That ATV is for EVERYONE. So, we all have to share."

I added, "I also got helmets for everyone, and you are not allowed to ride it without your helmet."

After my comments, Trevor took over, and said, "Rudy, you can always go first, but then I get to go next."

Eric piped up and said, "HEY, what about me? When do I get to use it?"

Trevor replied, "Dad, you can use it whenever you have work to do with it."

I looked at Eric and started laughing hysterically, joined by Heather.

But Eric was ready, and he responded to Trevor, "Well, since I am working ALL OF THE TIME, I guess that means I am the only one who will ever be using it."

Trevor realized his mistake, and replied, "NOOOOO!"

Now we were all laughing at Trevor.

Once the excitement died down, Eric went over with the boys to retrieve the ATV, and bring it down to the house. He first looked over at me, and me knowing what he was likely going to ask, I just said to him, "It should start right up." Eric nodded and headed over to the shed with them.

Heather and I went back inside the house. I wanted a moment by the fireplace with my tea. As I was heading back into the living room, Heather said, "That was so nice of you. Thank you. Really. Thank you so much. For everything. And not just the ATV."

I smiled and replied, "Sure. It makes me happy to do it. Truly, it does."

She headed toward the kitchen, giving me my short moment of rest and peace that I was seeking by the fireplace.

For some reason, randomly, I looked at the fire, then looked at the Christmas tree, and I said out loud, "Merry Christmas Frank." In a weird way, I felt his presence there, at that moment. I knew he would be delighted with everything that was going on at his farm. It warmed my heart.

I heard the roar of the ATV as Eric drove it over to the house. As Trevor had promised, he was letting Rudy go first. Eric helped Rudy put his helmet on, and then started giving Rudy basic instructions on how to drive it.

I had chosen the newest and best, but with safety and practicality in mind. It had ALL of the 'bells and whistles,' but it also was designed to have great stability for safety. Additionally, it had a huge amount of horsepower so that Eric could use it to drag logs, sleds, or anything else he needed to use it for.

It was nice seeing the kids so excited about it, but what made me smile just as much was seeing how happy and interested Eric was in the machine. He didn't just leave it for the kids to play with. He stayed out there and was messing around with it for his own enjoyment as well. I knew Eric had driven them before as a teenager, and he loved them. It was nice to see him get something for Christmas that I knew he would not only enjoy, but that would help him around the farm.

After a while, Eric came into the house searching for me, and said, "Don't you want to take it for a spin?"

I replied, "No, it's okay. I'm good. Besides, I don't want to wrestle it away from you and the boys."

Eric looked over at Heather, and she pointed at me and said, "What he said."

We laughed, and Eric went back outside with the kids. The three of them played around with that thing for a few hours before finally coming back inside, likely only because they were starving to death.

When it was nearing time for our Christmas feast; and all of us were gathered in the living room relaxing, I asked Heather, "What delicious surprise do you have in store for dinner?"

I truly didn't know. I had stayed out of the kitchen, and out of the way. Eric apparently didn't know either. Eric was always out in the barns doing chores, and today he had been outside all day with the boys playing with the ATV.

Heather, in a very matter-of-fact manner, replied, "We are having a goose."

Eric and I turned to look at each other at the same time. Once we locked eyes, we immediately started laughing.

At that point, I think we got each other laughing harder because we were also laughing at each other. We laughed so hard that we were nearly rolling around on the floor. Neither of us could breathe, we were laughing so hard.

Heather and the boys were watching our antics, and could not understand for the life of them what could possibly be so funny. They were looking at us like we had lost our minds. And we had. I had not laughed that hard since sometime before losing Frank.

Rudy started smiling and laughing, I think because he had never seen me laugh like that before.

Heather and the kids kept looking at each other, wondering what could be so funny that Eric and I were overcome to the point of no longer breathing.

I knew there would be no way for them to know. There was something about it that felt so great, that it was a private joke between just me and Eric. It gave me the feeling that Eric and I were truly reconnecting on a deep level, because it was something that went way back in time.

I am referring to the time when Eric and I were at farm camp, and to teach us a lesson about respecting the farm animals, and respecting life and death on a farm, Frank had harvested a goose on the farm that had become a 'pet' to us kids, even though one of the other kids had thrown a rock at it. Anyway, to teach us a lesson, Frank had roasted the goose for dinner one evening. The look on all of our face's that evening when we all realized it was our 'pet goose' for dinner, must have been priceless. None of us could eat it, except for a bite that we were all forced to take. We all learned to respect the farm animals, and respect where food came from that evening. Well okay, I guess you had to be there to fully appreciate it, but to me and Eric it was beyond hilarious.

The thought of having a goose for dinner again at the same exact farm, at the same exact dining table, was more than Eric and I could handle, as Eric and I certainly would have NEVER chosen to have goose for dinner EVER again after our past experience with Frank. HOWEVER, I knew that Eric did not have any geese on the farm at the time, and I knew this particular goose would be one that Heather had bought at the store. So, I knew this was going to be a perfectly edible and delicious meal. But still, the thought of it all brought Eric and I back to that time many years ago at the farm with Frank and his "goose lesson."

I can only assume that Eric eventually explained the entire story to Heather at some point afterwards.

It wasn't long before Heather announced that dinner was ready. We all filed into the dining room. Eric took his spot at the head of the table, I took my spot on the side near Eric, and Heather on the other side of Eric. Trevor sat next to Heather, and Rudy sat next to me.

Heather and the boys knew they had to wait for our version of the 'meal prayer.' I looked at Eric. Eric looked at me.

Then I said to Eric, "Go ahead."

Eric replied, "No. You do it."

I responded, "You are at the head of the table. It's your home."

Eric replied, "Doesn't matter. You are the one we all look up to, so you need to say it."

Eric and I stared at each other, as if it was a stand-off and stare-down.

Heather interjected, and said, "Oh my gosh you two, come on!"

Eric and I kept staring at each other, but we were getting close to laughing.

Heather finally looked over at me, and said, "I am the lady of the house, and I am declaring that YOU need to say it. It's for YOU to say on this day."

I knew I had just been defeated. Eric knew this also, and he laughed at me.

I responded, "Okay."

I took a breath and said, "WE ALL BELONG HERE!"

With that, we all dug in.

Heather assisted Trevor with some fixings he couldn't reach, and I did the same for Rudy.

Dinner was amazing! Heather had done such an extraordinary job. As we were all silently eating, I had an epiphany. I suddenly realized how much joy and happiness had filled the farmhouse.

I had many joyful moments in that farmhouse, especially with Frank, and certainly including on Christmas. But I could not think of a time when the house had been filled with as much joy as it was on this particular Christmas day.

I remembered how incredibly broken and despondent I was after Frank's passing. I remembered how lonely and empty I had felt inside that house, and specifically sitting at that dining room table all alone after having lost him.

Yet, here I was, on Christmas Day, with my "chosen family", the people closest to me in my life, all of us together, and everyone so full of joy, happiness, and full of life. The change in circumstances was beyond my comprehension. It reminded me that there is always hope, no matter how sad, depressed, alone, or hopeless you feel. There is always hope that things can change, and that things DO change. That is one guarantee in life; that things will always change.

I had so much gratitude for making the choices that I had made. "Giving" the farm to Eric was a huge sacrifice, which even I had questioned my sanity for a few times. But this Christmas Day showed me that my decision had been the correct and right decision. What was seen as a selfless act of kindness toward Eric at the time, was now an act that was rewarding to me in ways that I couldn't have ever anticipated.

I felt that I had created a wonderful family for the five of us, and I had filled Frank's house with more love and joy than could have ever been imagined. I 'did the right things,' and I felt it in the form of love, belonging, and my soul being at peace.

I guess you could say that the aforementioned epiphany was my own private silent prayer to myself that Christmas, during that wonderful meal. And if I ever had any doubts as to my own happiness, all I had to do was look to my right, where Rudy was seated. Whatever emptiness I may have felt previously was now gone. My cup was now filled to the brim, and it truly runneth over because of that boy. I knew Eric and Heather felt the same way about Trevor.

That was truly the best and most meaningful Christmas that we would ever experience, and we would reminisce about it each and every Christmas thereafter. We were most definitely living a meaningful life.

CHAPTER THREE
The Wedding

Winter had come and gone at the farm. We were in the initial phases of Spring, and there was a lot going on. Primarily, I had been working with Jonathan and our attorneys to achieve and finalize the adoptions of the boys.

My adoption of Rudy was going to be very straight-forward. Rudy's mom had signed all of the right papers before she passed away, and I already had permanent full custody. It appeared there would be no obstacles to me adopting Rudy.

However, the situation with Trevor was not as easy, since Trevor's father had left no specific instructions, nor a will as to what should happen with Trevor. While Eric had a temporary full custody order, he and Heather would still have to take 'the long path' toward a formal adoption.

Our attorneys were fully confident that the adoption would happen, but WHEN it would happen was in question. The attorneys suggested to us that one way to possibly make their case look stronger and speed things up, might be if Eric and Heather were to get married. Although it shouldn't matter, and perhaps ultimately wouldn't matter, the REALITY was that it would logically make things look stronger and more convincing if Eric and Heather were married, and then adopted Trevor TOGETHER.

I explained all of this to Eric and Heather, and they agreed and understood the logic. For this reason, Eric and Heather decided to do what was going to happen eventually anyways, and they decided to get married.

They were planning a Spring wedding to take place at the farm. So, in addition to everything else going on, there was also a wedding to plan for. Let us also not forget that the farm would be getting more sets of campers visiting at the start of the summer, which was right around the corner.

Meanwhile, my obligations with The Carlisle Trust continued, or should I say mine and Rudy's obligations with The Carlisle Trust. Rudy had become a permanent fixture at all of the meetings. He would be the first child to ever grow up inside The Carlisle Trust. Interesting experiment.

Rudy and I arrived at the Carlisle house for our latest meeting with Jonathan. I had something specific in mind that I wanted to discuss.

Once we were all settled in the meeting room, I launched right in before we got lost down some other rabbit hole. I explained to Jonathan that the previous summer we had a group of campers at the farm, and one of them, a boy named Marcus, had suggested that the high school have an Auto Shop program.

Like me, Jonathan was a bit of an intellectual, and an auto shop program was not the first thing that would come to his or my mind when thinking of new school programs. However, Marcus had inspired me, and showed me how critically important it was for schools to have alternative programs like that. Plus, everyone needs to have their car fixed eventually, and most of us have no clue how to fix cars. So, duh.

I told Jonathan that I was intending to speak with Mr. Bowman about instituting the Auto Shop program as suggested by Marcus, but that perhaps it would be best if Jonathan gave Mr. Bowman fair warning of my intentions first so that he could consider and digest the idea before being accosted by me.

Jonathan agreed, and I felt excited that I had begun to launch this new initiative at the high school, which would be in full swing by the time Marcus started into high school. It was important to me that kids see that their ideas were valuable, and that smart adults listen.

Once that item of discussion was behind us, Jonathan let some moments pass, and then he said, "This is awkward, and I am not sure how you will react to this, but I feel I need to keep you abreast of some chatter and discussions that some people have had with me."

I braced myself for anything, and replied, "What have we got going on now?"

He responded, "It's nothing bad. I have had some very influential people from BOTH political parties reach out to our office, and to me, and inquire as to whether you would discuss or entertain the idea of taking on a candidacy for political office."

I leaned back in my chair and rolled my eyes.

Jonathan said, "I know, but just let me finish. We have had offers of support and huge amounts of campaign funding if you were to consider a run for office, either for Governor or even for U.S. Congress."

This time, I not only rolled my eyes, but I sighed annoyingly and became very uncomfortable in my chair. I was having negative flashbacks of my stepfather's interrogation at the dinner table on Christmas Eve.

I looked at Jonathan and responded, "I am not a politician. I don't like politics. Politics divides people. My job is to bring people together by doing what's right, not by doing what's politically expedient. As long as I am the head of this organization, The Carlisle Trust will never become involved in politics, nor will it endorse one party over another. I, WE, are here to serve the people and the community in which we live, regardless of the politics or political preferences involved."

I stopped speaking and just stared at Jonathan with the most stern and serious expression I could muster.

Jonathan stared back at me, and replied, "When I was a child, I remember seeing an interview where George Carlisle was asked a similar question by a reporter. George gave the exact same answer that you just gave me now."

I smiled, and responded, "Well, there you have it."

I then looked directly at Rudy to be sure he was taking permanent mental notes on what I had just said. I could tell he was.

I looked back over at Jonathan, and said, "With all of that said, I have no problem with using our influence to partner with organizations, businesses, and individuals in order to accomplish our mission of making the lives of our citizens better."

I continued, "We must never forget that we are playing with George Carlisle's money. I didn't earn this money; he did. It is our duty to respect that fact, and uphold the ideals he stood for. Mr. Carlisle was a hugely successful entrepreneur and pro-business person who also believed in helping all people who needed help for whatever reason; and he believed in supporting education, and our kids. It is my solemn oath and duty to respect his ideals, and to use HIS money in accordance with his ideals. His ideals are my ideals, as if we were one. I will partner with anyone, or any business, who is in alignment with those ideals, for the purposes of accomplishing our mission of helping this community and its people."

I went on, "It is for this reason that I am contemplating ways that we can partner with organizations and businesses even much larger than we are, in order to further our leverage and ability to benefit people through sponsors supporting our efforts, similar to what we did with the Christmas festival by partnering with the trucking company and the toy company. If we do this effectively, there will be no cause, no project, and no challenge that we cannot take on and accomplish."

I finally stopped speaking. Jonathan had been pondering, and responded, "Interesting. Yes, perhaps we can take on sponsors who are much larger than us to help *us*."

I replied, "Yes, exactly. We don't need to be the 'big dog' who does everything on their own. We can get even bigger dogs to boost our ability and our reach."

Jonathan responded, "Got it. I will ponder all of this and keep my mind open to such opportunities."

I replied, "Perfect."

I stood up from the table to signal that the meeting was over. I felt that we had given enough ideas to contemplate, and I wanted to get Rudy home.

But after I stood up, I looked at Jonathan and said, "What I said at the festival, about making our community the greatest in the nation, or at least having that as a goal to shoot for; I was serious."

Jonathan responded, "Yes, I see that."

With that, I gave a wave and said, "Let me know if you need anything. We'll see you soon."

Jonathan waved and wished us well, as Rudy and I walked out of the room.

On our drive home, Rudy and I were both quiet, but when we were almost home, Rudy said, "I can't think of a better job in the world than your job."

I chuckled and replied, "I am finally realizing that you might be right."

It was time to set business aside for a while. The time had come to focus on the wedding. One morning, Eric, Heather, and myself were all sitting at the dining room table enjoying some breakfast treats and hot morning beverages. I was minding my own business, glancing at some notes for work, while also looking outside at the boys having fun in the front yard.

Eric and Heather started having a conversation amongst themselves about their wedding. They wanted to get married very soon because nice Spring weather had arrived, and because they wanted to hasten along the adoption process.

It seemed like they had both decided on a very small, if not invisible wedding ceremony. I was musing at the observation that the longer Eric lived at the farm, the more he was becoming like Frank. He had gotten to the point where he never wanted to leave the farm for any reason, and he had also become very private and anti-social.

Eric didn't want to have a wedding with guests. Heather seemed to agree and be okay with that. But they still wanted to make it special. They were debating about how many formalities to include, since nobody would be there to see them. They were debating and musing about if they should even dress up, or even have a cake, or even have anything at all. Their thinking was why bother going through the expense and trouble of it all if nobody was going to be there to see it.

It sounded like they only wanted me, the two boys, and both of their moms to attend. They started talking about how they wanted a few nice elements included only for the benefit of their moms being present.

I couldn't help but interject. I said, "You guys, this is your chance to have all of us, the kids, and your moms together in one place, at the same time. It might be a nice opportunity for some wonderful photos that you can always have and treasure."

I seemed to have their full attention, and they were taking on board what I was saying. They both contemplated, and then Heather replied, "Well, nice pictures means a photographer, and it also means outfit rentals, and a dress, or rather three dresses, including for the moms."

I responded, "Yeah, and if you're going to do that, then you might as well have a cake and flowers also."

Heather and Eric looked at each other.

Eric replied, "Yeah, and we don't have money for any of that."

I looked at both of them and purposely put a huge artificial smile on my face.

Eric rolled his eyes, and Heather quipped, "No! You've done enough already."

I responded, "I haven't done a wedding for you guys yet, though. That's something new!"

Eric laughed.

Heather looked at Eric and said, "I can't even deal with him anymore. He just keeps doing these things."

I interjected, "Because I like to. It's like my hobby. Are you trying to deny me my hobby?"

They both chuckled.

I paused, got serious, and said, "Seriously guys, this is how I see it. We are all a big family, and this is a great chance for all of us to get dressed up, have a wonderful event, and for all of us to get pictures that we can keep and appreciate for the rest of our lives. It's worthwhile. Most of all, it's very meaningful, and if it's meaningful, it's worth spending the money. Plus, meaningful things are my passion."

Eric and Heather looked at each other. Eric shrugged, and said, "The problem with him is that he's always right."

Heather shook her head and looked down at the table.

I said, "Good, I'm glad it's decided! Heather, you are in charge. You figure out what you want exactly, and I will be in charge of receiving the bills. This way we each have a job."

Eric responded, "What's my job?"

I replied, "Your job is to take care of all of the animals and accept all of Heather's choices."

Eric responded, "Sounds good."

Before either of them could argue with me further, I said, "Excellent! Meeting adjourned!"

I got up and walked out.

Heather got to work, and in no time at all, had a plan, and the event mostly all pulled together. She had chosen a dress for herself, as well as for the moms. She chose an outfit for Eric, and then outfits for me and the boys. She had a cake ordered, as well as flowers. A photographer for the event was booked. We had all of the elements for a great wedding, even though there would be only a total of seven of us in attendance. However, in pictures, it was going to look like quite a significant event, and that was the intention and idea.

It was decided that the two moms would arrive at the farm the day before the wedding, and stay for a night or two. Although I hated math, I was pretty good at it when I had to be, and I could quickly see that there were no bedrooms for the moms. Without putting Eric and Heather in the position of having to ask me, I offered that Rudy and myself would stay in the camper's cabin. This way, the moms could have my room and Rudy's room inside the main house to be with Eric and Heather. Rudy and I really didn't mind anyway. It would be kind of reminiscent for both of us to stay in the camper's cabin, since we had each stayed there during farm camp. I found it amusing how my son and myself had gone to the *same* farm camp and stayed in the *same* camper's cabin. It's weird how life can be.

Heather rushed everything along, and the day of the wedding was almost upon us. Well, except for one problem. And this "problem" made me almost roll on the floor laughing hysterically. Why? Because it was so basic, so simple, and so obvious, YET all of us had completely forgotten to consider it. WHO WAS GOING TO PERFORM THE CEREMONY?

Eric and Heather went into a panic once they realized this omission. My reaction was to simply make a phone call. Who did I always call when I didn't know what to do? The correct answer is: Jonathan. So, that's who I called. I explained the predicament and the problem. I asked him if he knew anyone who could perform the ceremony on such short notice.

Jonathan laughed. Then he got silent. Then he laughed again. I said, "Yesssss???"

He responded, "Believe it or not, I am able to perform wedding ceremonies." He explained that he had become a 'justice of the peace' as a result of his close ties with the community and the local town government. I guess he was a notary also. He was probably a whole bunch of things. This is why when one was lost and confused, it was a smart thing to call Jonathan.

I asked him if he would do it. He bent over backwards to say how honored he would be, and what a great pleasure it would be to do it for Eric and Heather. I filled him in on the details and thanked him profusely.

When I was finished with Jonathan, I went back to Eric and Heather, who were in a full meltdown about what to do, and if to just scrap everything and delay the wedding all together.

I exclaimed, "I fixed it."

Eric looked at me with his 'Eric look,' and replied, "Of course you did!"

Heather looked at me as if she didn't think it was possible to fix this issue so quickly and easily.

I said, "Actually, Jonathan fixed it. Jonathan is the one who fixes things. He's my 'fixer.' Because he fixes everything."

They both just stared at me. I continued, "Jonathan is a 'justice of the peace,' and he is coming to do it, if you approve of his involvement."

Eric and Heather both at the same time exclaimed, "YES! Jonathan is perfect! We would be honored if he would do it."

I replied, "It's a done deal. He will be here."

With that final piece behind us, Heather and Eric looked at me, and Heather said, "Eric and I each have something to ask you."

I replied, "Just name it."

Eric went first. He said, "Obviously, I would like you to stand with me as my 'Best Man,' if you will find it in your heart and your busy schedule to graciously offer yourself and your services for such a humble, yet important task."

I replied, "Well, my dear Sir, it would be my absolute honor, if not life-long dream, to be the one to offer my ever-lasting gesture of devotion; and I would be honored to serve you and your glory as your Best Man, if you will so allow it, dear Sir."

Heather rolled her eyes and started laughing. She just quipped, "You two guys.."

There was a pause, and then Heather went next. Heather said, "I am not as fancy as the two of you. I can't compete. So just let me ask if you would be willing to walk me down the aisle."

I thought for a moment, and replied, "That was more of a statement, and not a question."

Eric busted out laughing.

But Heather was not as amused.

I saw her expression, and immediately jumped over to her and hugged her, and said, "I'M JUST KIDDING! OF COURSE, I WOULD BE HONORED TO WALK YOU DOWN THE AISLE!"

Heather grew a smile on her face and responded, "Thank you!"

I replied, "My pleasure."

Heather then walked me, or rather me and Eric, through the series of events. She said that Eric, the boys, and the moms would be standing before Jonathan. I would walk her (Heather) down the "aisle" to Eric, and then Heather would take her place next to Eric in front of Jonathan. I would then slide in on the other side of Eric. Standing next to me would be Trevor, and then next to Trevor would be Rudy. Next to Heather would be her mom, and next to her mom would be Eric's mom.

Jonathan would lead the ceremony, and then he would ask for the rings. At that point, Trevor would come forward with the rings. Ahh yes, the rings. Eric and Heather got the rings on their own, and insisted on paying for them without my help. Thus, I was not involved with the rings at all, just for the record.

It all sounded nice to me. In the coming days, the wardrobe people were due to come out and drop off the outfits for all of us. I had previously had them come out and take all of our measurements. Heather had handled her own dress herself in town. The moms had stopped into the store separately at their convenience for their fittings. So, we were all set with outfits.

We were just waiting for the big day. The flower people and cake would arrive in the morning, and the photographer shortly before the ceremony. Everything was all set. It even looked like it might not rain that day. That was some good fortune right there.

Time passed quickly, and finally it was time for Rudy and I to move into the camper's cabin. We went in together with our suitcases. It felt weird. It was like I was going back to farm camp, except with Rudy as my campmate.

We both made a joke of running inside to claim the bunk we each wanted. FORTUNATELY, we chose different bunks. I chose my old bunk, and he chose his old bunk. I guess we were going to get along okay!

The moms arrived next. I gave Eric's mom a big hug. Although I never spent much time with her, it seemed like we had known each other forever, and had been through a lot together.

As far as Heather's mom went, it was my first time ever meeting her. I was very gentle and polite because of this, and she seemed very nice. I had heard all of the stories about Heather's household and the issues with her mom and dad. However, over the years, Heather's mom had separated from her dad, and she had really pulled her life together. For this reason, Heather and her mom had become closer, and thus why it was important to Heather that her mom be present and involved with the wedding.

We all had a delightful big meal that evening, compliments of Miss Davis, who offered to do it as her wedding gift to Eric and Heather. I managed to get Eric, who was sitting at the head of the table, to do the prayer, "We all belong here." I really wanted Eric to appear as the "head of household" to the moms, because that is exactly what he was. Luckily, he cooperated.

After a good night's sleep, and yes, I slept GREAT in the camper's cabin, we all got ready for the big day. The flower people arrived and did a huge arrangement, as Heather had requested. The cake arrived and was put safely in the dining room. The photographer arrived early and was ready for business.

Jonathan arrived, and it was a great opportunity for me to hang out with Jonathan as friends, rather than in a serious structured work setting. Jonathan had truly become a close friend of mine. I spoke with him more than any other person, except for maybe Rudy; so that had a way of making us close.

The moms got dressed, and then helped Heather get dressed. Jonathan and I ended up joining Eric and the boys. Eric already had the boys dressed, although I guess they did it on their own just fine. I asked Eric if there was anything he needed.

He replied, "Do you really think I would ask you for anything else at this point?"

I responded, "I'm your Best Man, so it's my job."

He just nodded and replied, "I'm good."

I decided to get mushy and reminiscent, and I said, "I can't believe you are getting married. Think of all the things we have been through together over the years; and now here we are, and you are getting married."

Eric thought for a moment and replied, "Stop it, or you'll make me cry in front of the kids and the moms."

I responded, "Yeah, me too. Okay. Well, just as long as you know I love you buddy, and I'm proud of you."

Eric got silent, and I could see his eyes turning red. I just pointed at him and said, "Ahh, careful!"

We both chuckled, and I decided to keep it light and relaxed after that, because IT WAS MY JOB to keep him relaxed before the ceremony. It was not my job to turn him into a wreck.

Heather's mom came downstairs, and announced, "She's ready!"

With that, everyone scurried outside to their appointed places. Jonathan got into his position, the moms in theirs, and the boys in theirs. I found myself inside all alone. Nobody ever told me at what point I was supposed to meet up with Heather, or retrieve her, or from where, or when. Ugh. Typical. My entire life I always found myself lost in these situations.

I decided to go upstairs and knock on the bedroom door and ask her what we were doing and how we were doing it. As soon as I got up there, she opened the door. She was completely ready, in her dress, and looked AMAZING. She had on a very classy, but simple white wedding dress with little aqua accents. It was then that I understood why our suits had aqua accents, and the mom's dresses were a shade of aqua.

Thankfully, Heather took control, and said, "Help me downstairs, and then once we are outside, you can escort me to Eric."

I did as I was told. I made sure she made it downstairs without a mishap to her or the dress. Once we were outside, I stepped next to her and took her arm, or rather, she took mine. There was no music, but I could almost hear music playing in my head. Once she took a step, I started walking her slowly to where everyone was standing. It was a beautiful, perfect day in the most perfect place in the world, as we were walking to the people who meant the most to us in the entire world. It felt so right. I was elated, and for a moment, one might have thought that it was me getting married, because I was beaming with such joy.

Once we reached the others, she gently dislodged her arm, and I smoothly slid over to Eric's other side. Jonathan started speaking. There were words said that Eric and Heather had provided. They were very personal to Eric, Heather, and the rest of us. They included the boys as well. I am going to allow those deeply meaningful and personal words and vows to remain private.

I will say though, that some of us had a tear or two from what was said. The kids were smiling and delighted that they were included in some of what was said. The moms were crying. Jonathan wanted to cry, but he kept it together, and was very professional, dignified, and graceful in how he presided over the ceremony.

Once all of that was said and done, Eric and Heather kissed. Everyone cheered.

Immediately after that, all of the formality of the ceremony lifted, and we all acted normally, and relaxed. We all hugged each other, and congratulations were given. I also made sure to compliment and thank Jonathan for what a superb job he had done. Everything Jonathan did was superb, no matter what it was.

We all went into the dining room to dive into the cake. "Dive" would be a very appropriate term for what happened. It was a beautiful cake, but we destroyed it. Heather and Eric had it in for each other, and they started to shove it in each other's faces with a vengeance. The kids started laughing hysterically. Then Eric threw some cake at the boys, and that started the boys throwing cake at each other. Jonathan and I hid around the corner while laughing at the antics. I wasn't safe, though. Rudy snuck up on me and shoved cake into my face. Don't worry, I got him back.

By the time it was over, it was clear to everyone that there would be no cake to eat. Luckily, we had plenty of other food, and again, compliments of Miss Davis, with perhaps a little backup help from

The Carlisle Trust staff who helped her out.

We had another wonderful meal, but this time it was informal, more like a picnic buffet. In case anyone was wondering about the farm animals, I had brought in some extra help to handle all of that. I used the same people that Frank had used the day of Mrs. Carlisle's funeral. No animal went unfed or neglected that day.

We all enjoyed the day, the occasion, the farm, each other, and the blessings that had been provided. Everything had been photographed, and there would be tons of pictures for us to treasure forever. A good time was had by all. We were all a family, and had been a family all along. But on that day, Eric and Heather became even more of a family, and they both glowed from it.

The next morning after the wedding, Eric's and Heather's moms left to go back home. Rudy and I moved back into the main house. Other than a bit of mess from all of the celebrations, things seemed to have returned back to normal. Well, except I knew there was going to be nothing normal about that particular day.

At lunchtime when we were at the dining room table eating, there were two cars that pulled into the driveway. To be specific, there was one large shiny red SUV, and then a car following it. It caught the attention of everyone at the table, and everyone was watching to see who was paying us a visit.

The person who had been driving the SUV got out of the vehicle, and immediately got inside the passenger side of the car that had followed it, and then the car immediately pulled away and drove off. We couldn't see or recognize the person who had been driving the SUV.

Eric and Heather looked at each other, and then they both looked at me. I chose to continue staring down at my plate. Heather asked Eric if he was expecting anyone, and Eric shook his head "no." They looked over at me and asked me if I was expecting anyone.

I replied, "I don't have meetings at the farm anymore, so it can't be for me. I'm just a guest here. I have no idea who you guys have coming and going from YOUR home."

Eric and Heather gave me a look, as they always did whenever I referred to the farm as *their* home, and not mine.

Heather looked at Eric and said, "Why would someone just park their vehicle in our driveway and leave? It makes no sense."

Eric replied, "Maybe they're coming right back."

We all continued to eat while Eric and Heather kept a close eye on the driveway to see if anyone would return. Nobody ever did.

Finally, Heather said, "People can't just park their vehicle in my driveway and leave."

I let a moment of silence go by, and then I said with a straight-face, with as boring of a tone as I could manage, "If it were MY driveway, I would go outside and check it out; and if they left the keys in it, I'd claim it as mine, since they left it in MY driveway."

After I said that, I received two very different looks from both Eric and Heather. Heather gave me a look of total confusion, like she thought what I was saying was ridiculous. Eric, however, gave me a very different look. Eric gave out a huge sigh, and then gave me his "Eric look." It was all I could do to keep a straight-face. Eric had figured it out. Eric knew exactly what was going on at that point.

But fortunately, Eric was a good sport, and he kept playing along.

I said to Heather, "Maybe you should go check it out, and see if they left a note on it or something."

Heather thought that was a great idea, and went out to look at the vehicle. Eric just stared at me, and I made sure to NOT make direct eye contact with him. Heather looked all around the vehicle, and then came back inside.

She said, "That is a BRAND-NEW vehicle. It even has temporary license plates on it. It's beautiful! Who in the world would just park a brand-new fancy SUV in our driveway and leave?"

Eric finally upped his game and decided to play. He replied to Heather, "Well, if it's brand-new and that nice, I'm keeping it if they left the keys in it."

Heather responded, "YOU CAN'T DO THAT, ERIC!"

Eric replied, "Why not? It's on MY property, and they just left it here with no explanation."

I jumped in and said, "Eric is right."

I paused, and then added, "Maybe see if it's unlocked, at least."

Heather was so confused, it was hilarious, but I remained completely calm, as if I was bored.

Eric said, "Okay, let's go."

Eric and Heather went outside, and I followed them. I waited just outside the door and watched.

Eric was trying to convince Heather to open the vehicle door, but she was resisting. Finally, he convinced her to open the door, and she did. She was still so confused. It was getting to the point where I was going to bust out laughing.

But then I saw Eric whisper something in her ear. She then threw her hands up in the air, put her hands over her mouth, and started crying. She came running straight at me, lunged, and gave me a big hug. She choked out the words, "IT'S ALWAYS YOU DOING SOMETHING!"

I finally gave myself permission to start laughing. Once she let go of me, I said, "Did you actually think I wasn't going to give you guys a wedding gift?"

Heather replied, "YOU DID! YOU PAID FOR THE ENTIRE WEDDING!!"

I responded, "Yeah, that was for the wedding. I still needed to give a wedding gift."

Heather and Eric were just shaking their heads at me. Then Heather said, "But it's huge and so fancy!"

I responded, "Yes, and that is not by accident. Consider this also as my payment for the carpooling you have been doing for Rudy. I wanted you to have a vehicle big enough for the carpooling. Plus, you guys needed a new vehicle."

Heather eventually walked back to the vehicle, but this time she got inside it, and started it up. She had a huge smile on her face. It was priceless.

Still standing near me, Eric said, "Thank you. Not just for the new car, but for making Heather so happy."

He added, "I am not sure if I'm more excited about the new vehicle, or about seeing Heather happier than I have seen her in a while."

I didn't say anything. It was just a happy moment to enjoy. I LOVED doing things for them. Buying things for myself was like a "nothing-burger," which is why I usually never did. But doing things for others always came with an epic feeling of great satisfaction and joy. I thrived off of it!

After the excitement of the wedding and the new vehicle calmed, life at the farm truly returned back to normal, and it was nice. I started using the back picnic table as my informal office again.

One day, I was sitting out there enjoying a cold beverage and reviewing Carlisle Trust papers, when Rudy came around the corner looking for me. He walked up to the table and took a seat.

I said, "What's up, Son?"

He seemed like he was gathering his thoughts, as if he had something to tell me, or was about to give some speech or presentation of some sort. I was intrigued enough to stop looking at my papers, and give him my full attention.

He responded, "Well, school is about to end soon, and I will be off for the summer."

I replied, "Yep."

He responded, "I know a lot has happened this past year, and that

EVERYTHING has changed."

He paused, and then continued, "BUT, I remembered something you said to me at the end of last summer."

I replied, "Yeah? What did I say?"

He responded, "You promised that if I did well in school, you would take me on a trip to California."

I chuckled and replied, "Yes, I did. You don't forget anything, do you?"

He quipped back, "Nope."

I was processing the implications of what he was saying or suggesting.

I replied, "So you want to go to California this summer?"

He responded, "Yeah. I was thinking we should go for the entire summer."

He added, "Because you have an apartment there and everything, we should stay. Then we can come back before school starts in the Fall."

I stared at him while my brain was twisting into a pretzel. I quipped, "Wow."

I looked up into the hills while I thought about his idea. I had honestly kissed California goodbye for the time being, and in fact, was about to have my car shipped home, and vacate the apartment.

My mind was bending and breaking. It had been a difficult process for me to accept and digest that my California days were over, and I had felt that I finally succeeded in doing that. I was firmly planted back home at the farm, and my focus was more on looking in a forward direction of remaining home, and perhaps moving us into the Wilkens house before next winter.

I looked at Rudy and said, "I was kind of looking forward to spending the entire summer at the farm. You don't want to stay at the farm?"

He hesitated, and replied, "I love it here. It's not about me not wanting to be here. I love the farm, and I love living with Trevor. It's just that I've never seen anything in my entire life. Before my mom died, the dream that I thought of every day was taking that trip to California with you. I wanted to see where you lived, and where you loved being so much. Plus, I wanted to go to Disney and things like that."

Rudy's argument was compelling. He was unknowingly starting to reignite the "California fire" within me again, which I had worked so hard to snuff out. The thought of being back in LA was very appealing to me. I truly loved it there. It was my alternate home where I felt "at home." Additionally, it was exciting to think of watching Rudy experience it for the first time.

I responded, "Let me consider this, Son. Eric was probably counting on me to help him with the summer campers and things. Plus, I need to check with Jonathan. It's not so simple anymore. Lots of people count on me, and I can't just run off and do whatever I want like I used to do."

Rudy replied, "Yes, I understand. But I'm just asking. We can do whatever you have to do. I'm still happy if we stay at the farm."

I responded, "I get it, Son. I understand. And I *did* promise you a trip. Let me work on this."

Rudy left me alone at the picnic table to contemplate, and that is what I did for a good half an hour. I thought about all of the pros and cons of going to LA for the summer. The more I thought about it, the more I wanted to do it. Rudy had awoken the sleeping lion. I never thought I would be able to spend a good stretch of time in LA again, and yet it seemed to be laying on a silver platter for me to take.

I decided in my own mind to leave it up to Eric and Jonathan. I made a deal with myself that if Eric and Jonathan both approved of the idea, then I would do it.

I went into the barn, where I found Eric and Trevor milking cows. I walked up to Trevor and said, "Can I have a few minutes with your dad, young man? I'll take over for you."

Trevor responded, "Yes, Sir."

He got up and left the barn. I don't think he minded much.

I started milking, and Eric said, "What's up?"

I replied, "Rudy just approached me out back, and called me out on a promise that I had made him last summer."

Eric responded, "What's that?"

I replied, "I had promised to take him on a trip to California."

Without hesitation, Eric responded, "Oh, nice. You should definitely do that."

I replied, "Yeah but he wants to stay out there for the entire summer."

Eric responded, "Oh, wow. Great!"

I replied, "Great? But that's a long time; and don't you need my help with the summer campers or something?"

He responded, "Nope."

I took some moments to think, and replied, "Is this your way of getting rid of me for a bit? Because if you need a break, I totally understand."

He quipped back, "NOPE, that's not it. In fact, it's the opposite. I don't want YOU to feel tied down or burdened by this place. This farm is MY responsibility. YOU need to have the freedom to go and do whatever you want. That was kind of our deal."

I thought about what he said. He was right, as usual.

I replied, "So, this is your official approval of us being gone all summer?"

He responded, "As if you need MY approval??" Then he laughed.

He continued, "If it makes you feel better, then yes. This is me supporting your plan to be in California for the summer. We'll see you in the Fall. Plus, if you made a promise to Rudy, you need to keep it."

There was nothing else for me to say at that point except, "Okay."

We finished milking cows and then went inside.

The next day, I called Jonathan. Since Rudy went to all of the meetings with me, I needed to call Jonathan about this so that I could speak with him in private about it, in case he had concerns that he was not comfortable airing in front of Rudy.

I told Jonathan about my prior promise to Rudy, and Rudy's suggestion about going to LA for the summer. I was expecting Jonathan to come up with some solid reasons as to why I should stay in town. He didn't.

His first comment was, "Wow, that sounds like a great opportunity for Rudy to get out of this town and travel a bit."

I paused, and replied, "So you are ready to get rid of me also? Eric already told me to go."

Jonathan responded, "Well, you will still be available to us, I assume?"

I replied, "Yes, of course. Same as when I was there before."

He responded, "It's fine. Go. Show Rudy the rest of the world. He needs to see more than just what we have here in this town."

Jonathan and I then discussed some of the logistics and implications that he would likely be involved in regarding all of this. It seemed fairly straight-forward, and Jonathan had no issues with it.

I was musing to myself about how the previous Fall, I had felt that everyone chastised me for being gone and sitting in California. But now, everyone was pushing me back out there. Weird how life works.

After dinner that night, I called Rudy into the living room to chat with me next to the fireplace. I asked him if he was sure he still wanted to be gone in California all summer. He confirmed that he definitely was. I told him that I needed to find us a place to live first.

He said, "I thought you had an apartment there already?"

I replied, "It's a dump, Rudy. And It's small. I need to find a proper home for us."

He responded, "When would we go?"

I replied, "As soon as school is over, I guess. So early June."

He responded, "Okay. I better go tell Trevor."

I replied, "Okay."

That prompted me to RUN into the kitchen and tell Eric and Heather, so that they knew before Trevor came running to them with the news. They were both very supportive.

Perhaps it was a great idea anyway, because Eric and Heather were newlyweds, and maybe it would be best for everyone if they had some time on their own without me always lurking around. Perhaps the universe was trying to arrange things how they should be. I think I had finally accepted this plan as being the right thing for everyone, and I was letting go of any hesitation or guilt I had about leaving again.

With Jonathan's help, I found a great short-term rental. It was a small house in Hermosa Beach, right where I wanted to be. It was three blocks from the beach, within walking distance of the pier, and it had two bedrooms, an office, and two bathrooms. It was available for us to rent for three months from June 1st to August 31st. And yes, it was expensive for just a three-month rental. But I justified it with the thought that I needed an acceptable place for Rudy, and that our time in California was going to be an important part of Rudy's development.

Our remaining time at the farm went by quickly. Rudy's school year ended, and it was time for us to make our way out to California. We all had one final dinner together, and it was bitter-sweet. Rudy was excited to go, but I was having anxiety about leaving the farm again. I always hated leaving the farm, and it always seemed like I was doing it too often.

We all spent a nice evening together out in the living room by the fire; but soon it was time to get to bed. For Eric, Heather, and Trevor, life would be going on as usual, and that meant early morning chores. We all ended up going to bed before it got very late.

In the morning, Rudy and I had a quick breakfast, compliments of Heather; and the car that Jonathan sent for us, arrived. We all said our goodbyes. After Rudy was in the car, I looked at Eric, chuckled, and said, "And here we are again, saying goodbye."

Eric laughed and replied, "Have a good time."

I responded, "Don't sell the farm while I'm away."

Eric laughed and replied, "You have made it legally impossible for that to ever happen." (True, thanks to Frank)

I responded, "We'll be back."

He replied, "You better be."

As I always did when leaving, I took one last long look at the farm, and all of its surroundings. Then I climbed into the car, and off we went.

I found myself in a limo service car, AGAIN, leaving the farm, AGAIN, and leaving home, as I had done countless other times. The more things change, the more they stay the same. At least this time, I would not be alone. I would be going with my best buddy.

Our flight was good, and as we were making our approach into LAX, it was fun watching Rudy look out the window onto the vast endless city of Los Angeles, or more accurately, the southern California area. On our way, I made sure to point out to him The Grand Canyon, Las Vegas, and Palm Springs. He was endlessly fascinated by all that he saw out of that airplane window, as it was his first time flying.

After we landed, we retrieved our luggage, and Jonathan had a car waiting for us. We drove directly to our rental in Hermosa Beach. We were able to get inside okay, and we inspected our new home. It was great! It was kind of small, a bit modest, and PERFECT! It was very clean, well-kept, and had everything we needed. I was very pleased.

The next day, we took a trip over to my old apartment. My plan was to pack up all of my personal belongings into my SUV, and then bring everything, and the vehicle, over to our new home. The rest of the things and old furniture, I would arrange to have picked up and donated, or thrown out. Then I would inform the landlord that this poor little college kid was OUT. I felt it was kind of clever that I already had a nice new vehicle waiting for me to use in LA. I was grateful that I hadn't jumped the gun and had it sent back home too soon.

When we arrived at my old apartment, we entered through the door, and I took a good look around at my surroundings. How weird. For a moment, it felt like I was back in my old life again. But Rudy standing next to me was a good reminder that I wasn't in my old life anymore.

Everything in the apartment was just as I had left it, and I was glad that I had thrown out all of the old food and garbage before I left last time.

I looked at Rudy's face, as he surveyed the place. He had the same look on his face that my mom likely would have had if she had seen it.

He said to me, "You lived in *THIS*?"

I laughed, and replied, "Yes. For three years. And I liked it."

He looked at me in disbelief. I kept laughing.

Then I said, "I told you it was a dump. That's why we got the house."

I could tell by looking at his face that he couldn't comprehend or imagine me living in that apartment for three years. It was really funny. And really, the funniest part was that I was dead-serious about liking it there. Crazy.

We got to work packing up my stuff. Neither one of us wanted to be there long. We moved quickly, and got everything I wanted to keep into my vehicle. When we were done, I left the keys on the counter and the door unlocked. I figured I would have the charity movers just come in and take everything, and then I would tell the landlord it was empty and that the keys were on the counter. I wanted to be done with it and never return again. That old life was over and done, and so was my time in that apartment. I hoped that some other young college kid might end up with it, and perhaps would enjoy their time there as much as I had.

We settled into our new temporary home quickly. We both felt very comfortable there. Because of how the house was set up, I ended up letting Rudy have the large bedroom suite. It made sense because the second bedroom and the office were right next to each other, such that you had to walk through the bedroom to get to the office. I didn't want to walk through Rudy's bedroom every time I wanted to go into my office. Plus, I wanted it quiet in the office, and that would not have worked with Rudy's bedroom right there.

Rudy, of course, was delighted that he had an entire suite to himself. It was the first time in his life that he had his own bathroom. I realized that I might have a hard time prying him out of there at the end of our summer stay.

We took a long walk, and I showed him the area so that he could find his own way around. Hermosa Beach was literally one of the safest (and smallest) cities in all of Los Angeles County. Kids could roam free without much worry, and they did so.

I made sure he knew where he was, where the house was, and the main "border points," such as the north end of the Hermosa Strand, the pier, and the south end of the Hermosa Strand. That was all bound by the 'green-belt' to the east, halfway up the hill toward Pacific Coast Highway (PCH). I told Rudy to always stay within those boundaries, and all would be well.

Our first dinner out was at my favorite pizza place, Paisanos

Pizza, near the Pier Plaza. They had the best New York style pizza, and I had eaten there, or done takeout, countless times before. Rudy loved its "beach vibe," and it became a favorite and regular place of ours to eat at almost every week.

Nothing in Hermosa was that fancy. That's how I liked it. If you wanted fancy, you could go up to Manhattan Beach or drive into the city. I liked the very laid-back vibe of Hermosa. It fit my personality, and I was hoping Rudy would learn to appreciate it as well.

Down from Paisanos, there was a little hole in the wall Mexican food place that I liked as well. Also, if you walked through the Pier Plaza, there were a variety of places that would change themes and names from time to time, but all were good. There was a very famous little place called The Lighthouse, where some very famous jazz bands had played live, including Ramsey Lewis. But the primary place that everyone knew of, was called Hennessey's. It was an Irish pub kind of thing, and was a great place for breakfast, lunch, or dinner. Additionally, there was usually an ice cream place around somewhere, and little gift shops, or surf shops. It was your idyllic California beach town. If any place was going to give Rudy a taste of southern California beach lifestyle, it was going to be Hermosa Beach, our home for the Summer.

It only took Rudy a few days before he was asking about going to Disneyland. I was excited to go with him, so we decided to go right away.

On our morning to go, he was up early, showered, dressed, and ready, all before my appointed departure time. I told him to wear very comfortable sneakers, because Disney meant lots of walking.

We took the 45 or so minute drive out there, and parked. We boarded the tram, and went to the gates. I had gotten us tickets beforehand, so we were all set with that.

I think I spent most of my time just watching Rudy's face. It was like Rudy had entered a world that he never had imagined even existed. He had never been to ANY amusement park, let alone Disneyland.

I led him up Main Street Disney and to Jolly Holiday bakery, where we could have a little breakfast. I spotted the perfect table and told him to go grab it, and that I would get our food and come back out to the table. I got us each a cinnamon roll and a couple of other things. That place was all about the frosted cinnamon rolls for me, but be sure to grab a gingerbread man cookie when they are in season.

After we ate, I started getting FastPasses for us. At that time, they had a great free FastPass system, so you could get passes for a few rides that you didn't want to wait in a long line for. In the process of doing that, I saw that the line for Haunted Mansion was short, so I jumped us into that line. I always loved that ride, especially in the middle of summer when I needed to escape the heat. It ended up being Rudy's first ride at Disney. He loved it!

We ended up doing Thunder Mountain Railroad, which was a roller coaster. For some reason, we both started laughing really hard on that ride, and it was tons of fun. I forgot who I was and how old I was. In that moment, I was a kid again, like Rudy. We couldn't stop laughing. I loved the goat at the top, and the sound it made; and most of all, I loved imitating the goat, much to Rudy's embarrassment and delight.

We of course did Space Mountain, and Rudy thought it was cool that it was in the dark. The secret I never told him was that the only reason I was able to go on it was *because* it was in the dark. I had a fear of heights, and I avoided the more intense rides, especially if heights were involved. But because Space Mountain was in total darkness, I was completely fine with it, and loved it. That became a favorite of ours.

We scooted over to Splash Mountain because we had a FastPass for it. We both wanted to go on it, but neither of us wanted to get soaking wet. Luckily, I knew a trick. If you ask the Cast Member to seat you in rows 5 & 6 (in the back), and then lift your feet up slightly while going down the drops, you can stay mostly dry. (You're welcome.) So, we enjoyed Splash Mountain without getting totally soaked.

We did Autopia, but shared a car. I let him drive. I kicked his butt at Buzz Lightyear Astro Blasters (I'm too competitive to let him win), and we ended up going on It's a Small World, because you have to go on that if you go to Disney. There were plenty of other little things here and there that we did as well. Disney is not about the rides though. Disney is about the little things and the small moments in between. It's about laughing with those you love while forgetting the outside world.

Speaking of in between, we had lunch somewhere within all of that chaos. We ate at this Mexican food restaurant right next to Thunder Mountain. There is an area where you can sit at a table right next to the Thunder Mountain tracks. That's where we sat. The Carne Asada was to die for.

Eventually, the day got away from us, and it started to get late. I wanted to show him California Adventure, so we left the Disneyland side, and went over to the California Adventure side. We didn't have much time, so we didn't go on any rides; but we walked all around.

I showed him the Grizzly water ride, and while we were standing there, one of the feral cats that lives there walked right up to us from the other side of the fence.

From there, we went into what was called Redwood Creek Challenge Trail, although it had changed themes and names a couple of times. It was a wilderness obstacle course type of thing for kids. Rudy had me chasing him all over the elevated netting that was strung up overhead. I began to feel my age. I wasn't 16 anymore.

But I was still able to keep up with him, though.

Eventually, we both grew tired. We ended up finally leaving, but we had such perfect timing that we were able to watch the fireworks as we were taking the tram back to the parking garage, and then saw the last bit of the fireworks from the parking garage. We drove home, and Rudy fell asleep in the car for the drive home.

Who had more fun, me, or him? I don't know. Perhaps me? I guess we will call it a draw and say that we both thoroughly enjoyed it, and I knew then that we would be making it a regular thing. I had already decided on the drive home to purchase annual passes for both of us. We could get good use out of them during our three months in LA if we went often, which we did.

After we had crossed off some of the major items on our list, such as Disney and the Hollywood sign, we settled into a very solid routine at home, and didn't leave Hermosa very often, except to go to Disney.

But one day, I ended up hearing or seeing something about a junior lifeguard camp that was being offered on the beach in Hermosa. It was for kids Rudy's age. I decided to enroll him in it, as a way of giving him a taste of lifeguarding, as well as getting him some exercise and hopefully giving him a chance to make some friends, even if our stay was only temporary.

He agreed to participate, and he seemed to enjoy it quite a bit. The instructors had the kids running around on the beach, similar to what Benny had done to me, except much more gently and reasonably. They taught the kids basics about being a lifeguard, and it was a great way for the kids to get a taste of the discipline involved, and the different skills necessary.

Rudy was inspired. He told me that he had interest in maybe becoming a lifeguard. I think part of the appeal for him was that I had been a lifeguard at The Lake. But being a lifeguard also coincided with his interest in swimming as well.

However, the best thing to come out of his experience at junior lifeguard camp was that he met a new friend that would become his "California best friend."

The boy's name was Wakeen. He was an incredibly delightful, smart, personable, and athletically talented young man. There was nothing not to like about that kid. The best part about him was his charisma. He was always funny and easy to talk with. I was encouraged by Rudy's choice in friends because of Wakeen.

As it turned out, Wakeen lived right in Hermosa Beach also. He lived with his mom and dad, but his dad traveled a lot for different things. Apparently, his dad was a retired NBA professional basketball star. Since I had zero interest in sports, especially basketball, I had no idea who his father was, or the significance. But I guess his father had been quite a big deal. I was likely the only person who had no idea about any of it, nor any interest. I was just delighted that Rudy had found a great friend and that Wakeen seemed like such a great kid.

I let Rudy hang out with Wakeen as much as he wanted. Sometimes Wakeen would be over at our house, but mostly, Rudy was over at Wakeen's house. I had no idea where exactly that was, so perhaps I deserved the "worst father of the year award" due to my ignorance in not knowing where my son was spending his time. But I DID speak with Wakeen's mom on the phone a couple of times, and we both seemed totally comfortable with each other, and with the kids spending time in each of our homes. Thus, I didn't worry much about it beyond that. With that said, I *would* eventually figure out where Wakeen lived.

One day, I was taking my regular walk on the strand to get my exercise. I knew that Rudy was hanging out with Wakeen. As I was walking up the strand, with the beach on my left and the mansions on my right, I suddenly heard someone yell, "HEY DAD!"

At first, I ignored it, but in the back of my mind it sounded like a very familiar "Hey Dad." Then I heard another "HEY DAD!" This time I stopped to try and figure out who was yelling that, and where it was coming from. I couldn't see anyone at first. I was looking all around. Then I looked UP and to my right. I couldn't believe my eyes. I had to do a double-take.

It was RUDY up on the second story balcony of one of those gigantic fancy mansions lining the strand along the beach. He was up there with Wakeen, and they both had huge grins on their faces. I just stared up at him, trying to process what I was seeing.

I yelled up to him, "WHAT ARE YOU DOING UP THERE?"

Rudy replied, "WAKEEN LIVES HERE!"

I responded, "OH."

I was surprised. I don't know why. I knew Wakeen's father had been a professional basketball player, but I guess I didn't fully process what the implications of that might be. Well, I knew after that. I made a mental note of which mansion it was so that I could remember where it was in case I ever needed to find my son.

I just yelled up towards him, "Don't forget to be home for dinner!"

Rudy replied, "Okay, Dad!"

Then I resumed my walk. I thought to myself, "Welcome to LA, where anything is possible, and you never know who you will meet, or what circumstances you may find yourself in."

I was very amused at how Rudy had never said anything to me about where Wakeen lived, or under what circumstances. He really didn't care. This is how Rudy has always been. Whether his friend lived in a cardboard box, or a huge mansion, it mattered not to Rudy; thus, he would have never thought of speaking about it to me.

After that, we ended up taking Wakeen with us to Disney a couple of times. His mom was very appreciative of this, and it was my chance to express my appreciation for her letting Rudy hang out at their house so often. She told me how they loved Rudy and it was no problem at all, and that he was welcome there anytime.

Rudy and I were both thoroughly enjoying our summer in California, but time was getting away from us, and our California holiday was heading toward its end. I think both of us started to panic about the fact that we would have to leave soon. It didn't really feel right to leave. We had fallen into a really good routine, both of us. It felt like home, and it was a lifestyle both of us were enjoying.

On top of that, Rudy had met Wakeen, and then had met Wakeen's other friends. Somehow, Rudy had become fully integrated into the culture and friend-circles of Hermosa, and in just a couple of months no less. I could clearly see that he was loving life, and he probably didn't want to leave.

It wasn't long before he voiced this verbally to me. We were walking along the strand on our way to have some pizza at Paisanos, and I noticed him looking at the ocean, the beach, the houses, the people, and taking in every morsel of life surrounding him.

Then he said it. He proclaimed, "Dad, I don't want to go."

I replied, "What do you mean? You don't want to get pizza?"

He responded, "No, I don't want to leave California. I know we are supposed to leave soon. I want to stay. We should stay."

I stopped walking, looked at him, and replied, "We sort of have to go back. We told everyone we would come back. Plus, you have school starting soon."

He responded, "Dad, you are always talking about doing what makes people happy, and living meaningful lives, and doing the right things, and all of that stuff."

He continued, "I'm happy here. I feel my life is meaningful here, and I can do all of the right things from here. AND, it seems the same is true for you, too."

His words gave me pause. I had not thought of it that way. If we were doing so well, then why change it? Also, if I was still living up to my responsibilities to others while being in California, then why did I NEED to change it?"

Rudy interrupted the silence and said, "I know you won't believe me, but I also FEEL, or SENSE, that there is an important reason why we need to stay. It has more to do with you than me. But I feel something is coming that we need to stay for."

I looked at him like I was wondering if he was pulling my leg at this point, and just saying things to convince me to stay. But then again, Rudy never did that. He was always honest and straight with me. I didn't know what to think, so I decided to just set it aside and not fully buy into it, but not argue with him on it either.

I thought for a bit, and said, "First of all, you would have to go to school here, and school here would be quite different than back home. Secondly, I would need to speak with Eric and Jonathan about this, because what I do, what WE do, affects their lives and the lives of others in big ways. Additionally, I don't even know if we can stay in our house here past the end of August."

Rudy replied, "I would be fine at the school here. I already know lots of the kids here. It would be the same as me going back home to school. In fact, I might know more kids here than I do back home."

He added, "And I know you need to check your other things, or with people that matter to you, and that's fine."

We reached Paisanos, and I said, "Okay. I won't promise anything, but I will consider this, and speak with those who would be affected."

He replied, "That's all I ask."

I rubbed my hands over my face, and replied, "That's *ALL* you ask??" Then I laughed.

He responded by just looking at me with his cute little grin. This kid was literally impossible to deny when he looked at me that way.

Mercifully, there were no further heavy subjects or bombshells brought up, and we both enjoyed our pizza.

The next day, I called Eric and explained the situation to him. Eric told me to do what was best for Rudy, because that is what he would do if he were in my position.

Then I called Jonathan, and explained the situation to him. Jonathan was a little more hesitant and thoughtful about the situation than Eric was, but he also expressed his support for whatever I felt was best. Jonathan told me that there really was no issue with me living out in California as long as something major didn't happen with The Carlisle Trust, where they needed me back home.

I thought about what Jonathan said, and I felt it translated to me being fine living out in California, but if something major came up, Jonathan would expect me to fly back home. That was obvious, and reasonable.

Then I had an idea. I decided to call Wakeen's mom. I confided in her what sort of work I did. She and I had a very nice conversation, and I felt comfortable asking her if she would be able to have Rudy stay with them for a short period of time if I ever had to fly back east in an emergency.

Without hesitation, she graciously offered to keep Rudy over there any time I needed, and for as long as I needed. She was so incredibly nice. I, of course, offered to do the same with Wakeen if ever needed.

With a backup plan in place to keep Rudy in school in California, even if I ever had to fly back home on a business emergency, I felt it was doable to stay in California. I also checked with the leasing agent for our house and inquired about extending our lease. The agent said it would be no problem at all.

It seemed there were no obvious issues preventing us from staying. Therefore, I informed Rudy that we could stay; but if there was ever a big problem, or if we ever HAD to move back home, he would have to accept it without argument. He agreed to the terms.

I immediately felt very rushed and behind the ball. School was about to start. I inquired with the school about enrolling him, and they required a copy of my lease and all of his information from the school back home. I had a lease that expired at the end of the month, so that was useless. I had to rush the leasing company to do the new lease for me so that I could provide it to the local school. Fortunately, I was able to negotiate a more reasonable monthly leasing rate that was more in alignment with a normal tenancy, rather than a "vacation rental rate."

With Heather's help, I was able to get all of Rudy's school records sent over quickly. In a very short period of time, I was able to extend my lease for the house and get Rudy enrolled in school. I guess things were going to work out okay.

He started school, and with Wakeen's help, it was very easy, smooth, and Rudy seemed to have no anxiety about it at all. Also, with him in school, I was able to get even more work done for The Carlisle Trust. It did seem that even staying in California, Rudy could do well in school and be very happy, and I was being more productive for The Carlisle Trust because I could give it more time and attention without any distractions or interruptions that I would have had if we had moved back home. Plus, we were not invading Eric and Heather's space all of the time, and I was sure that they had gotten used to having the entire house to themselves over the summer.

As for our new 'permanent' life in California, I felt strongly that I wanted Rudy involved in some kind of major activity other than just school and hanging out in Wakeen's mansion, although there was nothing wrong with that.

So, one evening at dinner, I said to Rudy, "I would like you to choose ONE activity to do, in addition to school. It can be a sport, art, music, or group, or academic, or anything. But I want you to be involved in something other than just school and hanging with friends."

Rudy thought for a moment, and replied, "Well, I wouldn't mind doing 'swim,' Dad; but they don't have that until I get into high school."

I found his choice intriguing and inspiring, and I responded, "Let me look around for what is available, and I will see what we can do."

I ended up doing some research, and there were TONS of options for swim lessons, swim teams, competing in swimming, and everything you could imagine. It was one of the things I loved about LA. There was EVERYTHING you could imagine available to you.

I inquired about this one program that was a swim team, part of a larger league, where the kids were coached to compete, and then would go to actual swim meets.

Rudy and I went to meet with the coach (program director), and he seemed like a very nice, but tough man. He reminded me of Benny. I think that is what sold me on him. Rudy was a bit intimidated by him, but Rudy loved the facility, and the other kids looked like they were having fun.

I enrolled Rudy in the program, and he started right away. I watched the first class, and the coach was very serious about training the kids to be competitive swimmers. It felt like this was the program you wanted your kid in if you wanted them to be on a high school swim team. I was very pleased. Rudy seemed to enjoy it also.

From then on, Rudy always had a swim function every Saturday. It was extra work and extra travel, but it was worth it. I felt it was really good for him, and I think he agreed. This meant we only had Sundays free for going to Disney or staying at the beach, but that was okay.

Rudy and I had found ourselves within a very busy, structured, productive, happy, and wonderful lifestyle in beautiful Hermosa

Beach in sunny California, while we were living a meaningful life.

CHAPTER FOUR
The Dork

When I was a kid in school, there was this stupid prank-game that we little idiots used to engage in. If we were in a crowd of people, one of us would yell, "HEY DORK!" We would then see who would turn around, as if they were responding to their name. We would then laugh at them for responding to 'their name,' "Dork."

Well, one Saturday, Rudy and I were up in Santa Monica for a swim meet that he was competing in. I had to get him there way in advance of the actual race times so that he could prepare with his team. For me, it meant a long wait with nothing to do, since he was not going to be swimming in his particular race for a few hours.

I decided to pass the time by going down to the Santa Monica Pier. For those who have never been there, it's an old-style pier, almost a very tiny "Coney Island" type of thing, for you East Coasters. They have a roller coaster, and lots of concession stands. It's a great place for teens to go on dates, and for adults to pass the time while their kid is at a swim meet.

So, I was strolling around the pier, and I stopped at the side railing to stand still for a moment, and look out onto the ocean. I was thinking about something, but nothing in particular, when all of a sudden, I heard a woman's voice from behind me say, "HEY DORK!"

Just like a stupid dork, I responded to it by turning around, as if I had heard someone call my name. I saw a slightly familiar woman standing a bit away from me, looking at me. For a moment, I thought I was seeing an apparition, or it was some kind of false illusion from my tired foggy mind.

The woman followed up by saying, "What? Are you too big and fancy now to remember who I am?"

It was then when I was certain of who she was. In my head, I still couldn't believe it, though. But logically, I knew who she was.

In my dazed confusion, I responded to her comment by saying, "No I'm not. I know who you are."

I was in total shock. It was Clarissa. She was my second girlfriend from high school, and my first true love. She also possessed ownership over the accolade of having taken my virginity. We were very much in love in high school, but she moved away at the end of my junior year. She had been one year ahead of me in school; so when she graduated, she and her family moved away for her to go to college, while I still had one more year left. I never saw or heard from her again.

I looked at her, and said, "I can't believe what is before my eyes."

She laughed, and replied, "You are still as charming and awkward as you always were."

I responded, "Yes, but less charming and more awkward these days."

She replied, "That's a lie."

She let a moment pass, and then she continued, "Don't worry, I've been stalking you for years, so I know that you became a big and fancy hotshot."

I responded, "Oh, is that so? Then if you knew about me, why did you never contact me, or say hi, or come visit me?"

She replied, "If I had done any of those things, it wouldn't have been considered stalking."

I responded, "Yes, true."

After a moment of silence, she changed out of her pleasant sarcastic tone that I loved most about her, and she became more serious, and said, "After seeing everything that has happened to you over the last couple of years, I don't know whether to say 'sorry,' 'congratulations,' give you a high-five, or give you a hug.

I responded, "I would prefer a hug."

We embraced, but in a polite way as casual friends might do. I then decided it was my turn to be a little obnoxious, and I said, "I assume you are here with your husband and five kids?"

She laughed, and responded, "There are no kids, but there was a husband that I had to get rid of."

I replied, "Sorry."

She responded, "Don't be. I tried it, and it didn't work. He lives in the area and we don't hate each other."

I replied, "Well that's good at least. I guess."

She responded, "What about you? I'm sure you've had women lining up, begging for you to propose to them."

I replied, "None. And if you've been stalking me, you already know this."

She responded, "True."

Then I thought of Rudy, and I said, "But I have a son."

Clarissa looked genuinely surprised. I guess that little bit of news was not in the local news stories that she had been reading about me.

She looked at me inquisitively, and responded, "So, no women, but you managed to knock someone up anyway? You always were a stud; it's just that nobody knew it except for me."

I laughed uncomfortably, and now she had me blushing. Never get into a sparring match with Clarissa because she always wins.

I replied, "No, he's not my actual son, but he's my son."

She laughed and responded, "You are also just as confused as you were back in high school. How cute."

I tried to clarify, and I replied, "I'm not even old enough to be his father, but he calls me "Dad," and I consider him to be my son. In reality, I'm more like a much older brother to him, but he's definitely my son, but he's not a little child, but he's my kid."

Clarissa was starting to laugh a little harder at me by this point.

I said, "I'm here now because he has a swim meet nearby."

She seemed sincerely intrigued, and responded, "Wow, so you're actually a dad."

I replied, "Yes, and it's my favorite job."

She looked at me more deeply, and said, "I guess it would be too mushy if I told you how proud I am of you with what you've done."

She continued, "I saw all of the pictures of you as the center of attention at Mrs. Carlisle's funeral. Then I saw how you took over the entire Carlisle operation and did those amazing things at Christmas time for all of the citizens. Impressive. If I had known you'd end up owning the town, I would have forgotten about college and never left you."

We both started laughing. I attempted to tone down her references by saying, "The situation is not exactly as you described, and I don't own the town, or much of anything really."

She just responded with, "Uh huh."

I realized how much time had passed since I had dropped Rudy off, and I said to her, "I should get back up to the swim meet so I don't miss my son's race."

I could tell that Clarissa was waiting to see what I might say, do, or suggest at that point.

I answered her silent question by saying, "Would it be appropriate for us to meet up for lunch or dinner sometime?"

She responded, "*Appropriate*? That's the best you got, Dork?"

I hung my head in shame and started laughing. My God, how I missed her!

Before I could try again with a different phrasing, she said, "Yeah, I think it would be 'APPROPRIATE,' but only if you can fit me into your very busy important schedule."

I replied, "Yes, I certainly can."

We then exchanged phone numbers. I gave her a quick hug, and I walked off. In fact, I walked off in the wrong direction due to being preoccupied with a multitude of thoughts and teenage flashbacks. Clarissa could see that I was walking down toward the end of the pier, instead of back to the street entrance. She 'waited for it,' and then saw me turn around to go back the correct way. As I passed her, she just stared at me and laughed hysterically. I couldn't help but laugh as well.

Fortunately, I made it back to Rudy's swim meet without further incident, and before his race.

As always, Rudy checked the bleachers to make sure I was there and watching. I cannot imagine what might happen if there were ever a time when he saw that I wasn't there. Would he even swim? Maybe not. Fortunately, I never missed a race.

As usual, he was one of the smaller kids in his race. I always enjoyed watching the other kids not familiar with Rudy look at him and dismiss him due to his size, only to see Rudy swim like a shark past them.

He didn't win every race. In fact, he usually didn't win. But he would very often come in second, or third at the worst. Regardless, none of the other kids would ever dismiss him again after they raced him once.

He would swim with incredible focus and intensity. He didn't have the strength of the other kids, but he moved his body faster, and would swim more technically correct than most of the other kids. It was like in those few moments, he would turn himself into a fish. It was always fun to watch him compete.

I would often see some parents in the stands looking bored to death. Some of them would be sitting there looking at something else, and not even watching their kid swim. They were just stuck there, waiting and hoping for it to be over. As for me, while I sometimes got bored waiting for Rudy's races, once his race was up, I would be totally focused on it, and I truly enjoyed watching him. There was no other place I would rather be in those moments.

After Rudy's meet, I waited for him outside. None of the kids ever got released until every race had finished, and even then, only after the coach spoke to all of them and released them. I preferred to wait outside in the fresh air and daydream about what had happened earlier with Clarissa. I still couldn't believe it had really happened. Seeing her again was all I could think about.

Rudy finally came outside, and we started walking to the car. I congratulated him on his third-place finish in the race, and in doing really well by approaching his 'personal best,' as far as his individual time went. He told me that he slipped a tiny bit on his start, and that he could have been much faster and should have gotten second or first.

We got to the car, and we started our way down the 405 Freeway back home to Hermosa. It was always slow-going. One needed to always bring their patience while driving down the 405 back home.

Due to the stop-and-go traffic, there was not much to divert my attention away from thinking about Clarissa. I am not sure how long Rudy was observing me for, but apparently too long, because he noticed my preoccupation.

He said, "Dad, you seem different somehow. Is everything alright?"

I replied, "Yeah, I'm fine. Never been better."

He responded, "Yeah, but something happened, I can tell."

It was literally impossible to hide much from Rudy. For lack of a better phrase, he truly was a mind-reader in its most literal sense. He would observe you very closely and intensely first, then his eyes would pierce your mind and body and do a full scan of your soul. At that point, there would be no point in trying to hide anything from him. It was easier to just tell him the truth.

I could see he was waiting for some kind of response that would answer his suspicions and curiosity.

I just said, "I went to the Santa Monica Pier before your race and something happened down there."

He replied, "What happened, Dad?"

I paused, hesitated, and responded, "I met a girl."

He immediately replied, "YOU met a GIRL?"

I responded, "Well, a woman. Yes. Sort of."

He replied, "Sort of what?"

I responded, "Well, she's not sort of a woman. She was, or is, definitely a woman. Not sort of. But yes, I met, well, not met exactly, I mean, I saw a woman. Well sort of."

Rudy was staring at me and wouldn't let me out of his tractor beam.

He replied, "Dad, you aren't making any sense."

I responded, "Yeah, that's what she said also, well, I was like that with her also. I always was, actually."

He replied, "Always was? I don't understand."

I responded, "Well, I knew her from before. And I was always that way, kind of, when I was that age. I guess I'm still that way, aren't I?"

Rudy just stared at me, partly out of amusement, and partly out of concern.

He broke his silence, and replied, "This girl, I mean woman, has made you crazy."

I responded, "Yes, she always did."

He replied, "ALWAYS DID?"

I responded, "Yeah, I knew her in high school. Well actually, she was my girlfriend in high school."

Rudy exclaimed, "SHE WAS YOUR GIRLFRIEND!!??"

I responded, "Yeah. 10th and 11th grade."

Rudy quipped, "WOW!"

I responded, "Yeah, exactly."

He just kept staring at me, except now with less concern, and with much more amusement.

After some much-needed moments of silence, he ruined it and said, "What are you going to do with *this* woman?"

I replied, "DO WITH?"

He responded, "Yeah. Did you talk to her?"

I replied, "Yeah, of course. We talked quite a bit."

He responded, "About?"

I replied, "Just catching up. Normal things."

He responded, "Did you hug her or kiss her?"

I replied, "RUDY! Come on, give me a break!"

Rudy kept staring, waiting for an answer.

I said, "We hugged. Obviously. We hadn't seen each other in a long time. Since we broke up, well sort of. We didn't actually break up. Actually, we never officially dated. But she was my girlfriend for a couple of years, though."

Rudy responded, "Huh?"

I replied, "Never mind. We just hugged as friends."

He responded, "And then what?"

I replied, "And then what, what? That's it."

He responded, "What are you going to do now?"

I replied, "About what?"

He responded, "ABOUT HER!"

I sighed in an exasperated way. I was getting exhausted from his interrogation.

I paused, and replied, "I might call her. I *will* call her."

Rudy responded, "And then what?"

I replied, "What? I might meet her for lunch or dinner or something."

He responded, "YOU'RE GOING ON A DATE WITH HER!!?? YOU ARE DATING THIS PERSON, WOMAN?"

I replied, "No, I'm not *DATING* her. I am going to meet her for a meal."

He responded, "That's a date, Dad. That's what a date is. When you meet a girl for a meal. It's a date."

I replied, "Okay."

A long silence went by. I was wondering if Rudy was having an issue with all of this.

I said, "Do you have a problem with this?"

He replied, "No. But I just think I should know if you are dating a woman. I mean, it's supposed to be you and me. It *IS* you and me. So, if you are dating someone, I should meet them and approve of them first."

I responded, "WHAT? APPROVE OF THEM FIRST?"

Rudy knew he might have overstepped his bounds, and he didn't reply. But he started to sulk. I started to feel bad. I reminded myself that Rudy was my first priority before anything else, and anyone else. In a way, Rudy was right. Well, he wasn't. But in my heart, he was right.

I thought for a few more moments, and then said, "So basically you want to meet her first before I 'date' her, or go on a date with her."

He replied, "Yeah, I just want to meet her. I'm not telling you what to do, or that you can't do anything, Dad. I'm just saying I should meet her."

I responded, "Hmmm, okay, maybe. I can ask her."

Rudy just stared at me, and replied, "Okay."

He was completely silent the rest of the way home, and once we got home, we went right to his room. I knew I was in the doghouse with him. SIGH.

Some folks will understand my position, and others won't. Yeah, he was just a child, and I could do what I wanted with whomever I wanted. BUT, IN REALITY, when you have a kid like Rudy, are a single parent, and you have a very close relationship with your child, it's not so simple and easy as people think. What THEY think MATTERS, regardless of what old-fashioned views a person might have on the issue.

Well, it was Chinese food night, and after it was delivered, I retrieved Rudy from his room. We sat down at the dining table to eat. He wouldn't look at me.

I said, "Rudy, I'm going to ask her if she will meet both of us together first, you and me."

He seemed a bit conciliatory, and replied, "Okay, that's fine."

He added, "What's her name?"

I responded, "Clarissa."

He replied, "Is she nice?"

I laughed, and responded, "No, she's mean actually. And that's what I like about her."

Rudy looked at me like he wasn't sure if I was kidding or serious. Of course, I was both.

I paused, and said, "Rudy. Do you really think that anyone I WOULD LIKE would be someone that you would not like? Think about it."

Rudy paused, and replied, "True. I like all of the people you like."

I responded, "Exactly."

Finally, we were finally able to enjoy our dinner now that Rudy seemed to have let go of his temporary resentment against me. I figured out in my mind that I would wait until Rudy went back to school on Monday, and then I would call Clarissa in the safety of total privacy.

The rest of the weekend came and went, and Rudy was off to school Monday morning. I resumed my normal weekday routine of handling all of my Carlisle Trust issues in the morning while Jonathan and his staff were still in their normal workday. I always had the 3-hour time difference to contend with, and it wouldn't be fair to them for me to make them stay late at work just because of my time difference. Thus, I made sure I did my work with them in my mornings so that they could leave at 5:00PM their time.

This meant that I could handle all of my personal business and household chores after lunch; and could also enjoy a great lunch, and sometimes even a nap, all before Rudy got home from school. After school, he would either spend time with friends, or do homework, and I would go for my walk before arranging for our dinner after that.

I was pretty busy on Monday, but on Tuesday I decided to make myself call Clarissa. I was very nervous to call her for some reason; I'm not sure why. Clarissa and I were boyfriend/girlfriend for two years. Why was I nervous? It made no sense. It was like I was back to square-one with her, as if I didn't even know her.

I suppose I was a bit nervous about trying to explain to her about the issue with Rudy. Since she didn't have kids, she likely would not understand my predicament, and perhaps this would end things before they even had a chance to begin.

I contemplated calling her, and worked up my courage to do so. I felt like I was 15 again. I called the number she gave me, and she answered.

I said "Hi," along with who I was.

She laughed. She replied, "You think I don't know you, and you have to introduce yourself like I'm some kind of business associate?"

I laughed, and responded, "I don't know. Maybe you forgot about me and don't remember my voice."

She replied, "I never once in all of these years forgot about you, and I doubt I ever could."

Fortunately, she couldn't see that I had started to blush and melt in my chair. I started to try and speak, but couldn't get words out.

She said, "So you just wanted to call me to see if I would know your voice?"

I replied, "No."

She giggled.

She responded, "WELLLL???"

I replied, "I, of course, wanted to arrange a time when we could possibly meet."

She responded, "Oh, of course, good Sir. When might that be *appropriate*, dear Sir?"

I laughed.

I finally just let go. I said, "Look. I was going to ask you out to dinner, but I have an issue here."

She responded, "Oh? And what would that be?"

I replied, "My son Rudy found out that we had met, and he kind of freaked out. He doesn't have an issue with YOU, but he is insisting that he meets you first before I meet you alone."

Clarissa started laughing.

Thank goodness she was having a sense of humor about this, because I wasn't. I was listening to myself speak, and it sounded pathetically ridiculous.

After she finished laughing, she responded, "So, your little man won't let you see me until he meets me first, and approves me. Is that it?"

I chuckled uncomfortably, and replied, "Pretty much."

She immediately responded, "That's really cute. I would love to meet him."

I breathed a sigh of relief, which I think Clarissa must have heard.

I replied, "So I am changing things up. I am wondering if you can come to lunch down here in Hermosa Beach on Sunday?"

I continued, "Rudy has school all week, and then he has 'swim' on Saturday. We are free Sunday. We can have lunch at a restaurant at the pier? Once he is satisfied, he will likely run off to one of his friend's house's or back to our house alone after lunch; and then you and I can take a walk on the strand, alone."

She responded, "That sounds fine. I've been to Hermosa before. How about I meet you at the Pier Plaza at 1:00PM?"

I replied, "That would be great. I'm thinking we will eat at Hennessey's. Do you know it?"

She responded, "Oh yeah, I love Hennessey's."

I replied, "GREAT! We'll be there."

We ended our call, and I felt extremely relieved.

That night at dinner, I said to Rudy, "WE have a date on Sunday with Clarissa."

He replied, "Oh, okay, cool. Where?"

I responded, "Down at Hennessey's."

He replied, "Okay."

After a pause, I responded, "So this means that if you don't hate her, you need to let us go for a walk after lunch, okay?" (Was I really asking permission from my child as to whether I could go for a walk with a woman?) (Yes, I believe I was.)

Rudy replied, "Okay, Dad, it's a deal. I will want to go see Wakeen anyway."

I responded, "Okay, good."

Sunday, 'Date Day,' arrived, and I decided that Rudy and I should walk down to the restaurant a little early so that we could get on the list for a table on the roof. Although I liked eating inside and downstairs because it was quieter, I thought it would be more fitting and impressive to eat on the roof, with Clarissa being there and all.

We walked down to the restaurant, and when we arrived, I asked the hostess about a table for three on the roof. She said it would only be about fifteen minutes.

About five minutes after that, I could see Clarissa walking down the Pier Plaza toward us. She could already see me. She had a smile on her face.

She walked up to us, and she and I hugged. I could see Rudy carefully observing and inspecting every facet of the hug.

Immediately after the hug, she turned 100% of her attention to Rudy.

She said, "You must be Rudy!"

Rudy replied, "Yes, Ma'am."

Clarissa responded, "Oh, please don't call me 'ma'am.' It makes me feel like an ancient old lady. Call me Clarissa, okay?"

Rudy nodded his head.

Clarissa then said, "Wow, you are even more handsome than your dad."

Rudy smiled in a slightly amused and embarrassed way.

Clarissa said, "Rudy, I just bought this keychain because it caught my eye. What do you think of it?"

It was a keychain with a surfboard attached to it.

Rudy replied, "That's really cool. It has a surfboard. I love surfboards. I might learn how to surf."

Clarissa responded, "Well, here, why don't you have it. I don't surf, so you should have it."

Rudy took it with a giant smile on his face, and replied, "Thank you, Clarissa."

I then saw that the hostess was ready for us. I said, "I think our table is ready. Shall we head up?"

They started following me, as I was following the hostess. We got seated up on the roof.

Clarissa said, "This is really nice."

Rudy replied, "Yeah, my dad and I eat here a lot, but not usually on the roof. I think my dad only wanted to eat on the roof because you're here."

Clarissa started laughing while I was cringing within myself.

Clarissa looked at Rudy and said, "Rudy, you seem like you are very protective of your dad and always looking out for him."

Rudy nodded his head and replied, "Yeah, he is my only dad, so yeah."

Clarissa and I laughed.

Clarissa responded, "Well, I really respect that about you. You know, a long time ago when I was in high school with your dad, I used to do the exact same thing you are doing. I used to be very protective of him and watch who he was talking to."

She continued, "Sometimes your dad could be a little naïve about people, and he got confused often. Does he still get confused, Rudy?"

Rudy had this huge grin on his face, on the verge of laughing, and he replied, "Yes, he does. That's why I have to keep an eye on him all of the time."

Clarissa responded, "I totally understand, because that's what I used to do for him a long time ago. We had the same job, Rudy." Then Clarissa put her hand up for a high-five, and Rudy slapped her hand with a giant smile on his face.

Right then, the hostess came, and we ordered our food after discussing the menu for a minute. As the hostess was walking away, Rudy asked Clarissa, "What was my dad like in high school?"

Clarissa, making direct eye contact with Rudy the entire time, replied, "Your dad was complicated. He was kind of a nerd, but he was also very funny and interesting. He could be very quiet, but then sometimes he would never stop talking. But he was always smart, and he was always saying all of the right things to all of the people around him."

Rudy nodded and responded, "He is still exactly like that!"

I just kept sipping my iced tea, praying that nothing horrible would be said by either party.

Eventually, our food came, and I was hoping *that* might slow the chatter down just a tad. It didn't.

Clarissa and Rudy kept talking back and forth. It was apparent that *they* were the ones on a date, and I was the third wheel. At the same time, it was amusing and heartwarming to see how well they were hitting it off. Clarissa was playing the situation perfectly, as

Clarissa was highly skilled at doing; and Rudy was completely enthralled and taken by her.

Clarissa said, "So Rudy, I understand you swim competitively, is this true?"

Rudy replied, "Yeah, I'm on a swim team. I love swimming. I drowned and died once a long time ago, but my dad saved me, and now I want to be the best swimmer I can be."

Clarissa looked at me in a shocked, concerned, and curious way.

I quipped, "Long story."

Clarissa looked back at Rudy and said, "Well maybe sometime your dad will let me come to one of your swim meets. I would love to watch you compete."

Rudy's face lit up, and he replied, "I would love that!"

There was a gap in the conversation, and then Rudy dropped the bomb.

He looked at Clarissa, and said, "Why did you and my dad break up in high school?"

I visibly cringed. I knew something like this was coming, but I wasn't sure whether it would come from Rudy or Clarissa. Clarissa did not even miss a beat.

She looked right at Rudy, and responded, "We broke up only because I had to move away for college. I was very in love with your dad. If I hadn't moved away, we would have stayed together."

Both Rudy and Clarissa looked over at me. I nodded, and said, "True."

That explanation from Clarissa seemed to really satisfy Rudy. That was clearly his big "test question," and I think Clarissa had passed.

After that, Rudy slowed down on his questions, and we were able to make some small talk. We finished eating, and I paid the bill.

Just before we stood up from the table, Rudy looked at Clarissa and said, "I hope you still like my dad because I want to see you again."

Both mine and Clarissa's hearts were melting. Clarissa replied, "Of course I like your dad, and I would be delighted to see you again."

Rudy smiled, and we stood up and left our table. Clarissa was able to give me a huge amused smile without Rudy seeing.

Once we walked down and out of the restaurant, I looked at Rudy and said, "Okay Rudy, you have my permission to go hang out with Wakeen now if you want."

Rudy rolled his eyes, and annoyingly replied, "YES, DAD. I KNOW."

Clarissa started laughing because I think she had figured out what was going on.

Clarissa said, "It was really nice to meet you, Rudy."

He replied, "It was nice meeting you too, Clarissa."

I gave Rudy a little wave and a smile. He started walking up the strand, but he looked back at us about three times before he was out of sight.

Clarissa started laughing.

She said, "Did I pass?"

I replied, "He wouldn't have left us here alone if you hadn't."

We both laughed.

I continued, "Let's just give him a few minutes to get ahead of us, and then we can walk up to the end of the strand where Manhattan Beach starts, and we can turn around and walk back to wherever your car is."

Clarissa responded, "Sounds good. Lucky I brought my walking shoes."

I replied, "Always, when in Hermosa Beach."

After a couple of minutes, we started walking.

Clarissa said, "I love the way he looks at you. You mean *everything* to him."

I replied, "Well, he means everything to me."

She responded, "I see that. But before I met him, I had assumed that your only focus would be The Carlisle Trust. I know how important your job is with that."

I replied, "Yes, that's my other major concern and love, but it comes after Rudy."

I added, "I have several 'loves' in my life."

Clarissa responded, "What else?"

I replied, "The farm. I absolutely love the farm back home."

She responded, "Then why don't you live there?"

I replied, "Because I gave possession of it to my best friend, Eric."

She responded, "Why in the world would you do that if you love it so much?"

I paused, and replied, "Well, because I wanted Eric to have it more than me. It's hard to explain."

She responded, "Well, it sounds like you care a great deal about Eric, also."

I replied, "Definitely. He's been my best friend through everything."

She paused, and responded, "It sounds like you have a lot of 'loves' in your life. Maybe you don't have room for any more."

It was then when I realized my mistake. *THIS* is why I never dated and was not capable of dating. I would ALWAYS say the wrong thing without realizing it.

I replied to her, "I have PLENTY OF ROOM for more loves. For example, I currently have room to spend time with my very first and only love of my life."

She smiled, and responded, "Are you really telling me that there was nobody else after me?"

I replied, "Yes, I'm really telling you that. And the fact I am saying that is embarrassing and shows you how pathetic my life has been."

She started laughing.

Right about then, we were approaching the mansion where Wakeen lived; and I had a strong suspicion of who I was going to find peering down from the balcony. Sure enough, as we got to the mansion, I could see a little face Rudy with his big eyes peering down upon us. I decided to not acknowledge him, and to not point him out to Clarissa. I didn't want to encourage Rudy, and I didn't want to have to spend a bunch of effort explaining to Clarissa why Rudy was in one of the largest and nicest strand mansions spying down on us. I just walked right on by, although I could see Rudy through the eyes on the side, back, and top of my head. I'm certain he would have kept watching us until we were too far up the strand for him to see anymore.

Clarissa and I walked a little further up, and then decided to turn around and walk back. I think both of us were starting to feel some tension and anxiety, because we knew the 'date' was coming to an end.

There was more silence during our walk back. I couldn't think of anything to say other than, "I will walk you all the way to your car. Where are you parked?"

Clarissa responded, "Oh, have you had enough already?"

I replied, "No."

She responded, "Well what if I don't want to leave?"

I replied, "Well then you would have to move into our house, and we would have to explain to Rudy how you are living with us now, after only one date."

We both laughed.

Clarissa responded, "I guess I better not push my luck with Rudy so soon."

She added, "I'm sure me coming to your house will require an entirely additional interview and security screening by him."

We both started cracking up.

I replied, "It might."

She ended up telling me where she was parked, and that's where we went. Once we got close to her car, she pointed out which one was hers. We walked up to it along the sidewalk, and we both stopped.

She looked at me and said, "So is this where you tell me how delightful I am, and then I never hear from you again? Because I think that's normally how these dates work."

I replied, "Nope. This is where I tell you that I'm going to engineer a way for us to have a date *alone*, without the Rudy police. You just have to be patient and let me work my magic and figure this out."

She responded, "What happens after you are able to work your magic? I remember you used to work your magic after dark at the park. Are you still just as magical?"

I didn't know how to respond to that, as usual. But it was a good signal of where things could go.

I took that reliable military intelligence, and I responded, "What happens is that I will invite you over to my house, and we can have a more relaxed date at my home."

With a mischievous smile she replied, "I'm usually not allowed over to a boy's house after only one date, but I will sneak out and try it anyway."

Then she said, "Are you then going to cook for me an amazing gourmet meal?"

I laughed, and replied, "You wouldn't want to eat anything I cook. We can order anything you want, though."

She responded, "Then perhaps I will do the cooking. Do you even have a pan?"

I laughed and replied, "Funny you should ask, because the first thing I bought after everything happened was a new fancy pan."

She started laughing and responded, "I know you are being

completely serious, is the funny part."

I replied, "Yes I am."

She responded, "I bet you still like Mexican food, don't you?"

I replied, "Some things will never change."

She nodded and responded, "Okay."

A moment went by, and she said, "I will wait to hear from you then."

I replied, "Yep, soon."

She stood there looking at me. After an awkward silence, she said, "I know it's only the first date, but you're allowed to kiss me, you know."

She didn't need to ask me twice. I went in for a very nice and gentle "first kiss."

She smiled and said, "You are such a polite boy."

I chuckled and quipped, "Not always."

She nodded her head and responded, "I know. I remember plenty about the naughty boy."

Before it got more awkward, she climbed into her car. I waved at her, and then watched her drive off. Wow, did it just get really hot in the kitchen, or was it just me?

Rudy came back home right before dinner. We sat down for dinner, and I was very preoccupied. I'm sure he noticed.

He broke the silence, and said, "I really liked Clarissa."

I replied, "Good, I'm glad."

He responded, "So, I'm just saying that I approve of her and you can date her."

I laughed. He was so serious when he said it. I didn't reply.

Then he said, "I'm hoping you DO date her."

After a couple of moments, he added, "So, when will you see her again?"

I replied, "Soon."

Fortunately, he changed the subject and started talking about some new game that he and Wakeen were playing on their gigantic TV screen that apparently took up most of one wall. I was kind of listening, but not really listening. I couldn't get Clarissa out of my mind.

But then Rudy said something that was the most delicious music to my ears. He said, "Dad, is it okay if I have a sleepover at Wakeen's house next Saturday? We already asked his mom and she said it was okay with her if you said it was fine."

With *that* question, Rudy had regained 100% of my attention. I responded, "So you want to spend the night at Wakeen's this coming Saturday, this coming weekend?"

Rudy replied, "Yeah, Dad, that's what I said. Is that okay? We want to play games and watch movies in their theater room."

I responded, "Theater room?"

He replied, "Yeah, they have a movie theater inside their house. It's like a real movie theater, except smaller and more fancy."

I shook my head, and responded, "Wow. Okay, well that sounds great to me. You can tell Wakeen's mom it's fine with me, and to call me if she needs to speak with me, or if I can do anything."

By the way, that was another thing I loved about living in Los Angeles, and specifically Hermosa Beach. People would say what they wanted about me back home, as far as our position and status in the community went, but in California, I felt poor, and I loved it. I'm not sure why this was. But it just seemed like back home I had a lot of eyes on me, and a lot of pressure. In California, I was a tiny fish, and I felt no pressure, no eyes on me, and I could just relax as a small fish.

Among Rudy's friends, we probably lived in the smallest house, *and* we rented on top of that, while they all owned their houses. Granted, I could have bought us a really nice house there if I wanted to, but it didn't make sense to do so because I was afraid that we would have to leave at some point. I didn't have a very good record of being stable in one place for very long. Thus, renting was by choice and the smart decision. Besides, I loved this little house we were living in.

The next morning, Rudy was off to school and I was back to my routine schedule, which included working on all of my Carlisle Trust tasks. However, I took a moment at lunch to call Clarissa.

When I phoned, she answered, and I said, "You can always tell a guy is pathetic and desperate when he calls back the very next day after the first date."

She replied, "You are neither of those things; but calling the next day definitely shows eagerness. Are you eager?"

I responded, "Very eager."

Before she could respond more to this ridiculous banter, I said, "There has been some magic."

She replied, "Oh? You worked your magic that quickly?"

I responded, "Yep. Well, Rudy worked it for me. He is the magical one."

I continued, "Rudy claims that he is spending the night at his friend's house this coming Saturday night."

Clarissa replied, "Oh. So when the cat's away, the mice shall play?"

I responded, "Yes. It's kind of like when mom and dad are leaving for the weekend, isn't it?"

She replied, "Yeah, parents should never leave when they have teenage children 'in heat' home alone."

We both laughed.

I responded, "So, might you possibly be available for some kind of appropriate, or better yet, inappropriate meeting at my home on Saturday night?"

She replied, "Sounds like too much fun to miss. I assume you haven't learned how to cook in the last 24 hours and still want Mexican food?"

I responded, "No, and yes, please."

She replied, "Okay, I'll stop at the store on the way there. I'll be there between six and seven?"

I responded, "Perfect. And bring your jammies. There might be a slumber party."

She laughed and replied, "I always come prepared; you should know this."

I responded, "Can't wait. See you then."

We ended our call. I was excited! I literally hadn't done anything like this since, umm, since, well, I was with Clarissa as a teenager, when we would have all-night picnics in the park, or when her parents would go out of town for the weekend.

After I had locked in my weekend, I tried to focus on the week ahead, and actually do some work. After a day, I settled back down into my routine and was acting like an adult again, rather than a love-sick teenager.

Saturday morning came, and Rudy and I went to his swim event for that weekend.

On the drive home from that, he asked, "What are you going to do while I'm having my sleepover at Wakeen's house?"

If I hadn't said it before, I will say it again. I couldn't get away with anything with Rudy. He always knew if something was going on. He would read my mind, or just 'know' something was going on. There was also no point in trying to evade him, or God forbid, lie to him. The only option was to tell him the truth.

I sighed, and replied, "I have a date with Clarissa."

He smiled and responded, "Yeah, I figured that."

After a moment, he added, "It's okay, Dad. I like her."

I replied, "Yeah, so don't be coming home unexpectedly. You are not allowed to crash this date."

He laughed and responded, "I know, Dad. I won't be back home until at least after lunch on Sunday."

I replied, "As long as you are home for dinner. It's going to be you and me for Sunday dinner as always."

He responded, "Okay."

We got back home from his swim event, and he took a shower and got dressed for Wakeen's. He packed a backpack, and told me he was leaving.

I said, "Okay, be careful. You can call me if there is a problem, okay Son?"

He replied, "Okay. See you tomorrow, Dad."

We hugged, and he left.

After Rudy left, I cleaned up around the house and I took a shower. I was nervous enough to the point that I tortured myself over what I should wear. Part of me just wanted to wear sweatpants to keep it very informal and relaxed like in the old days. But part of me thought wearing sweats was too suggestive, and that I should wear normal street clothes, like jeans. But then part of me thought I should be dressing nicely in business casual attire. I ended up compromising, and went with the normal and comfortable street clothes. I needed to try and act normal, and not like a dork.

After I had gotten ready, and was not embarrassed by the condition of the house, I heard a knock at the door. It was Clarissa. She walked inside looking very beautiful and quite informal, as if we both were of the same mind about things. She had bags of groceries to make dinner. I took the bags from her, and we went into the kitchen.

She said, "Wow, this place is really cute. Did you buy this house?"

I replied, "No, we're just renting. I'm afraid to buy anything out here because my life is back home, and I don't want to buy something, and then have to move back home in a year, or even less."

She responded, "Makes sense."

I replied, "Plus, the bedroom situation here is a little weird. So even though I love the house, I am not sure I would buy it with this bedroom setup."

I started leading her on a tour. She had seen the living room, dining area, and kitchen. I showed her where the bathroom was, and then led her toward the back of the house where my bedroom and office were. I showed her how you had to walk through my bedroom in order to get to the office.

I said, "See, this is the awkward bit, and this is why this room is *my* bedroom."

I then showed her Rudy's room.

She said, "OH MY, so Rudy has a large full bedroom suite."

I replied, "Yeah, because I had to take the other one. That's why it's not ideal, but I love everything else."

She responded, "So your little man rules the roost. Nothing happens without his approval, and he *ALSO* resides in the main suite."

I chuckled and replied, "Yeah, funny how that happens."

She responded, "He means everything to you. I think that is really sweet; and it says a lot about a man when they love their child that much."

Clarissa then asked how I ended up with Rudy. I think she had heard bits and pieces, but I gave her the medium-length version of what happened. I knew she was curious, because in reality, I was not old enough to be Rudy's dad. I was more like Rudy's much older big brother if we went strictly by chronological age. But the dynamics of my relationship with Rudy had always been 100% father/son. I suppose lots of people wondered how I could have a son that was so old, or rather how I could have a son that age, with me being as young as I was. Oh well. People could wonder.

Clarissa and I went back into the kitchen. She started preparing dinner. Looked like chicken enchiladas to me! Yum!

While she was making dinner, she said, "So, how do you take care of a child while not cooking?"

I replied, "We order out mostly. Sometimes we walk down to the pier and eat there. Once in a while I might cook something in my fancy pan if I'm forced to."

She responded, "So he doesn't get home-cooked meals much, or ever?"

I paused. I felt like a horrible father, maybe?

I replied, "Well, when we stay at the farm back home, we get home-cooked meals every day. But here in California, it's like I described. He likes it."

She responded, "A growing boy like him needs lots of unprocessed foods, vegetables, and a good mix of foods."

I replied, "Are you applying for the job? I might have an opening for a cook?"

She smiled and responded, "Oh Babe, I don't *APPLY* for jobs. I am always recruited from the very top."

I chuckled and replied, "I don't doubt it."

She then asked me how I was able to live in California, considering my position back home. USUALLY, I was very private about my personal situation, and my business situation, but Clarissa knew much of the inside-deal. She knew what I had, who I was, and maybe even a good guess of roughly how much I might be worth, as well as where I was at in life at the moment. There was no point in being uncomfortable, evasive, or playing coy with her. I guess you could say that she was sort of like Eric, as far as my comfort level in speaking freely.

I explained to her that I didn't know what was going to happen, and that we were still in California only because Rudy wanted to stay. I told her that if anything ever happened back home, I would have to go back, and that everything back home had priority. I was trying to convey to her that I took my position at The Carlisle Trust very seriously. She had not been to the Christmas festival and seen what happened in person, but she read about it in news stories. She knew of the emerging importance I played in the community.

I could tell during our discussions that her wheels were turning in her head, as if she was trying to figure out where I was going to end up living. The thing is, I didn't even know where I was going to be living; so there was no way for her to know, either.

When dinner was ready, we sat down to eat. It was my turn to ask about her. She told me about her marriage that had ended in divorce. Then she told me that she had become even closer to her parents, and remained in the area because of her parents.

She told me that she went to school for nursing, and was working at Cedars (hospital), and that she was able to choose her own hours most of the time.

It occurred to me that I had already had a full date with her, and I didn't know any of this about her until this moment. It made me feel bad. I made a point of spending the rest of the evening just asking about her.

In summary, she had built a very solid life for herself, despite having gone through a divorce. She had her family nearby and a great flexible job.

Later on, and deeper into the conversation, it was revealed that she lived with her parents. I think she was embarrassed to tell me. She had moved in with them after her divorce, and just never left because it was working out so well.

This explained why she didn't invite me to sneak over to *her* place at any point. I asked her if her parents knew that she had seen me again. She indicated that they knew, and that they were delighted.

I recalled that I had a great relationship with her parents in the past. They liked me when I was 16 and 17, so why wouldn't they like me now? At least *that* was going to work out okay.

I offered that I should come up sometime and take her and her parents out to dinner so that they could see me again and meet Rudy. She agreed that was a great idea.

After dinner, we cleared the table, and I told her to just leave the dishes. I could take care of all that the next day. No need to spend our time together dealing with that. Instead, we moved to the couch. I had everything set up like we used to have it when we were teenagers. I made sure there were lots of pillows and a couple of blankets. We liked to lounge together sharing a blanket or two.

We settled into the couch together, and she said, "I feel like I'm a teenager again."

I replied, "I know. It's great."

We started reminiscing about old times. We had some good laughs, and some good excuses to cuddle closer together.

Eventually, she said, "Where does all of *this* lead to?"

I knew what she meant. I replied, "Maybe we're just picking up where we left off, as if you never left for college."

She responded, "Yes, except you somehow got yourself a child while I was out at the store buying a loaf of bread."

We laughed.

I replied, "True. But Rudy loves you."

She responded, "Really?"

I replied, "Yes. He for real told me that he hoped I would date you. It was like he was making sure I was going to see you again, as if insisting that I did."

She responded, "Oh, that's sweet."

I paused, and then said, "Look. I know my life is different now. I know *I'm* different. I know my entire life situation is completely different. There is nothing about my life that is the same anymore. I'm complicated, and my life is complicated. I can't hide it, and I can't change it, nor would I want to."

I continued, "So, I would understand if it is all too much for you. This is why I don't date at all. I know it's pointless to try. But what I do know is that being with you makes me feel wonderful things that I forgot I could feel. And I know I feel good with you. For me, that is enough to want to be with you."

I went on, "So for me, this is all very simple. Yes, my life is very complicated. But my feelings are very simple. I'm either happy, or I'm not. And with you, I feel happy. So that's all there is to consider for me. So, really, all of this is up to you because I have already decided. And I decided that I like this, right here, and right now."

I stopped talking because I knew I was rambling. She looked over at me, and it seemed like she might cry. I didn't think I had said anything very touching. I was just being brutally honest and straight-forward.

After a few moments, she responded, "Listening to you talk that way reminds me of what I always loved about you. You have always been so certain of yourself and your feelings. You have such a gentle authority about you. It's like strength and power wrapped up in a gentle and kind sandwich bun."

I replied, "So I'm basically a sandwich."

We both laughed. I added, "I suppose I'm full of bologna and you think I am a bologna sandwich."

She responded, "No. More like prime beef with just the right amount of secret sauce."

I replied, "That sounds a little better, anyway."

There was a long pause while we just snuggled together on the couch.

After a while, she said, "When we were kids, I was the one who led. But I think now, you are the one to lead."

I responded, "Yes, Ma'am, whatever you say, Ma'am. I always did as you said, and I will continue to do so."

She giggled.

It was getting late. Neither of us were 17 anymore. We were starting to get tired, and we didn't want to get 'too tired.' Therefore, we moved 'the party' into the bedroom. She used the bathroom, and I got ready for bed as well.

What happened next will remain private. But I felt like I was 17 again, and I hope she did as well.

The next morning, we both woke up at the same time. We looked over at each other in bed and laughed. We decided no words were needed, or wanted at that point. We both got up, used the bathroom, and got dressed.

Clarissa cooked us breakfast. It was an amazing breakfast. It reminded me of how much I missed eating breakfast at the farm. She and I had a nice breakfast together, along with some hot tea. She was a tea drinker just like me.

She asked me when Rudy was coming home. I told her he wouldn't be back until after lunch. I suggested to her that we go for a walk on the strand along the beach. She agreed. We went out for the walk, but I made sure to lead us in the direction that would not put us walking past Wakeen's house.

We had a very pleasant walk. For the first time (ever?), or since I was a teenager, I felt like I had a 'partner' to enjoy my Sunday morning with. After our walk, we came back home and had leftovers from the previous night's dinner.

After lunch, she knew she needed to go, and we were both bummed. I think we both were really enjoying each other.

I said to her, "Let's organize a family dinner."

I continued, "What I mean by that is let's have you over when Rudy is here, and let's have a real legitimate family dinner with the three of us. How does that sound?"

She replied, "It sounds wonderful. Like a real family."

I responded, "Yes. Like a real family. Yes. A family."

I could tell she liked that, as did I.

She gathered up her things, and I walked her outside to her car. We knew that we had already said everything we wanted to say. We just hugged and kissed, and then she left.

I went back inside and started cleaning up. When I picked up the blanket from the couch, I could smell her. I held the blanket to my face for a good full minute, just smelling her. I felt something deep inside my heart that I thought was either dead or no longer existing. Yet, there it was. Again.

Rudy eventually got back home. He asked me how it went. I told him it was wonderful, and that Clarissa wanted to come over and cook us dinner sometime.

I said, "How would you feel about that, Son?"

He replied, "You mean like we would have a real dinner, like a real family?"

I chuckled and responded, "Yeah, like a real family."

He smiled, and replied, "I like that."

He then told me that he didn't sleep the entire night, and he was going to his room to rest.

I said, "Okay, Son."

He went into his room, and I went back over to the couch to smell the blanket. Was I in love again as I had been when I was 17? Or did I never fall out of love? Either way, it felt like I had gained another very important person in my life. With so many blessings and wonderful people in my world, I felt that my life had become more meaningful than at any other point, and I was smiling because of it. All of it was because I had made promises, and kept promises. That was resulting in me living a meaningful life.

To further enjoy this series, "Living A Meaningful Life," be sure to check out the other books in the series below:

Book #1: **The Bench:** *Living A Meaningful Life*
Book #2: **The Farm:** *Living A Meaningful Life*
Book #3: **The Lake:** *Living A Meaningful Life*
Book #4: **The Favor:** *Living A Meaningful Life*
Book #5: **The Promise:** *Living A Meaningful Life*
Book #6: **The Sacrifice:** *Living A Meaningful Life*
Book #7: **The Challenge:** *Living A Meaningful Life*
Book #8: **The Wedding:** *Living A Meaningful Life*
Book #9: **The Crew:** *Living A Meaningful Life*
Book #10: **The Substitute:** *Living A Meaningful Life*
Book #11: **The Graduate:** *Living A Meaningful Life*
Book #12: **The Nemesis:** *Living A Meaningful Life*
Book #13: **The Proposal:** *Living A Meaningful Life*
Book #14: **The Estate:** *Living A Meaningful Life*
Book #15: **The Heir:** *Living A Meaningful Life*
Book #16: **The Renaissance:** *Living A Meaningful Life*
Book #17: **The Shelton:** *Living A Meaningful Life*
Book #18: **The Ramone:** *Living A Meaningful Life*
Book #19: **The Spare:** *Living A Meaningful Life*
Book #20: **The Gala:** *Living A Meaningful Life*
Book #21: **The Commencement:** *Living A Meaningful Life*

Book #22: ***The Bank:*** *Living A Meaningful Life*

Book #23: ***The Dean:*** *Living A Meaningful Life*

Book #24: ***The Key:*** *Living A Meaningful Life*

Book #25: ***The Hospital:*** *Living A Meaningful Life*

Book #26: ***The Lieutenant:*** *Living A Meaningful Life*

Book #27: ***The Flashback:*** *Living A Meaningful Life*

Book #28: ***The Promotion:*** *Living A Meaningful Life*

Acknowledgments

Thank you Sarah Delamere Hurding for your editorial assistance, encouragement, and endless support.

Thank you to David Ferrari for your special support of the series.

Thanks to all of my clients and benefactors who have supported my mission of helping people become greater, stronger, more self-empowered, enlightened, and free of pain. Thank you to all of the kind people in the world.

A special thanks to Enya and KOS Music for their musical inspiration.

I would also like to thank Janet Manley Atkins for her support.

ABOUT THE AUTHOR

Brian Hunter is an American author best known for his book series, *Living A Meaningful Life*, and his numerous self-help books, including his Best Sellers *Heal Me, Rising To Greatness, Surviving Life,* and *EVOLVE*. Brian had a rural upbringing, surrounded by small towns, farms, lakes, and the peace of nature. Eventually, he moved to Los Angeles, California, where he began a career in acting and modeling. Brian was in a wide range of TV and movie productions with small bit parts. He then began spending his time mentoring and counseling young people and adults who suffered from depression and other struggles. Ultimately, he began his writing career. After writing several self-help books, Brian answered his magical calling to start writing the *Living A Meaningful Life* series. The series has turned out to be one of the largest family saga series ever to be written in recent history, and continues to grow and expand. Brian's goal is to use the successes from his works to fund philanthropic programs to benefit children, schools, and communities.

www.brianhunterauthor.com

ALSO, BY BRIAN HUNTER

Living A Meaningful Life is an epic book series, with numerous installments, that will change your life. We are all capable of doing extraordinary things. We must only decide within ourselves to *BE* extraordinary. The *Living A Meaning Life* book series is a powerful story, and journey, of one such 'family' who dared to be extraordinary. By looking past their own obstacles in life, and choosing to always 'do the right things,' they became extraordinary within themselves, and this resulted in them doing extraordinary things that changed the lives of everyone around them, and their community. The main characters must navigate life struggles, both personal, and community oriented. They do so by 'doing the right things,' through exhibiting integrity, decency, generosity, and compassion. Life is never easy, people make mistakes, but there is nothing that can't be overcome when we have the courage to do what we know is correct and true within our soul.

Heal Me is a powerful and touching book that will pull at your heartstrings, give you practical advice on overcoming a variety of life traumas, and will put you on the road to recovery and healing. *Heal Me* examines such issues as the death of a loved one, loss of a pet, suicide, anxiety, addiction, life failures, major life mistakes, broken relationships, abuse, sexual assault, self-esteem, living in a toxic world surrounded by toxic people, loneliness, and many other issues. This is a self-care book written in a very loving, practical, and informative way that you can gift to yourself, family, young people, and friends, as a gesture of love, support, and hope.

Rising To Greatness is a self-help book that takes you on a step-by-step transformation, from the ashes of being broken and lost, to the greatness of self-empowerment, accomplishment, and happiness.

This book includes such topics as developing your sense of self, eliminating fear from your life, mastering your emotions, self-discipline and motivation, communication skills, and so much more.

Surviving Life: Contemplations Of The Soul is a unique and powerful book full of compassion and empathy, which combines the issues of what hurts us the most, with thoughts and advice meant to empower us toward happiness and independence. *Surviving Life* is medicine for the soul. It guides us through our deepest pains and weaknesses, and leads us to a place of self-empowerment, inspiration, strength, and hope. The topics covered are raw, diverse, and very practical. *Surviving Life* includes many subjects, and answers many questions, such as, "What is your purpose on this planet," "When you think nobody loves you," "How can you feel good," as well as practical advice on battling depression, suicide, and figuring out who you truly are. *Surviving Life* is a practical and contemplative manual for people of all ages, and the perfect book for gifting to those who need guidance and love.

EVOLVE is a cutting-edge, unique, powerful, and practical personal transformation self-help improvement book, which examines human life and all of its issues from a unique futuristic approach with a touch of humor. A selection of topics include: healing from personal losses and traumas, coping with sadness and depression, moving past fear that others use to control, manipulate, and abuse you, clarity in thinking, advanced communication skills, evolving your relationships, exploring the meaning of life, how everything in the Universe is connected, developing your psychic ability, and a little discussion about aliens possibly living among us. Yes, there is everything, which is all directly tied back to your own personal life.

LIVING A MEANINGFUL LIFE
BOOK SERIES INSTALLMENT SYNOPSIS

This is a series for adults, but has many themes, stories, and lessons, that would be enjoyed by a teen audience as well. Through its down-to-Earth, emotional, and touching storylines, the series shows the importance of developing self-empowerment, and a person's own deep character, through mentors, self-work, and 'soul-families.' The main theme is that of always 'doing the right things,' as a way of living a meaningful life. All installments within this series feature characters of all ages, from children to older adults. The series is neutral on religion and politics. There are tears of sadness, tears of joy, and lots of laughs. This is a series that changes lives.

Book #1, The Bench, is an important book that lays the foundation for the series. This installment provides the background for important mentors and characters featured in the series. This installment covers much of the main character's childhood, and provides important lessons learned, as well as a number of the back-stories referred to later on in the series.

Book #2, The Farm, is the more "juvenile" installment of the series but is a critical book that provides the background on the most important mentor of the series, as well as many of the back-stories for the series. In this installment, the main character is a young teen. This is also a "coming of age" installment, where the main character realizes the meaning of leadership, and the importance of having a mentor.

Book #3, The Lake, is the installment where the main character transforms from a teenage child to a highly dynamic teenage young adult. This installment is a major turning-point in his life. His destiny is decided in this installment, but he doesn't know it yet.

Book #4, The Favor, is the most pivotal installment of the series. Everything changes, and the main character's future is laid out before him. Highly emotional and intense installment. The main character is now a young adult, and a new future star of the series is introduced.

Book #5, The Promise, is the 'relief' installment after the intensity of Book #4. The main character must accept his new life, and live up to his promises and obligations. The new rising star of the series begins to become very prominent.

Book #6, The Sacrifice, reminds us that things can always change in an instant. This installment tests the resolve of the main character, as he must draw upon the lessons taught to him by his mentors, as he faces his greatest challenge yet.

Book #7, The Challenge, is the next most pivotal installment, where the previously rising star of the series solidifies his prominence as THE star of the series. This installment exhibits the power that people can have if they dare to rise up and soar like an Eagle.

Book #8, The Wedding, gives us what we have been wanting and waiting for. But in addition to that, this is the "coming of age" installment for the young star of the series, who all of a sudden, blossoms into a young man with his own independence and ideas, as most older teenagers do. The young star continues to surpass all expectations.

Book #9, The Crew, gives us a closer look at Rudy's huge inner-circle of friends, and their antics. This installment is another high-point in the series, as it chronicles Rudy's growing success, but also a very emotional event which rocks his world. How Rudy handles this "event" will prove him worthy of his destiny. A highly emotional installment.

Books #10 and above: You will have to read them to find out. The journey continues to become even greater and more meaningful. The best is yet to come. The journey will never end.